CU00961370

To Hull And Back

Short Story Anthology 2019

Copyright © 2019 Christopher Fielden. All rights reserved.

The copyright of each story published in this anthology remains with the author.

Cover copyright © 2019 David Whitlam. All rights reserved.

The cover features the congenial countenance of Alan MacGlas.

First published on Hulloween, October 31st 2019.

The rights of the writers of the short stories published in this anthology to be identified as the authors of their work has been asserted in accordance with the Copyright, Designs and Patents Act 1988.

All rights reserved. No part of this publication may be reproduced, stored in a retrieval system, or transmitted in any form by any means, electronic, mechanical, photocopying, recording or otherwise, without the prior permission of the publishers.

You can learn more about the To Hull And Back short story competition at:

www.christopherfielden.com

All characters in this publication are fictitious and any resemblance to real persons, living or dead, is purely coincidental.

ISBN: 9781695078178

INTRODUCTION

Welcome to the sixth To Hull And Back short story anthology. I hope you enjoy all the fabulous fables contained within this tantalising tome of humorous delights.

My competition 'reading, judging, procrastinating and having a complete 'mare making decisions because the stories are all too good' trip was very enjoyable this year, but more challenging than ever – there were *many* brilliant stories entered into the competition, all exhibiting different qualities. The shortlisted stories contained in this book are the most imaginative of those tales, weaved with care, skill and just a smattering of wizardry.

The anthology opens with the three winning stories of the 2019 competition. These are followed by the three highly commended tales from the runners-up, in alphabetical order (based on story title). After that, the other 14 shortlisted stories appear, again, in alphabetical order.

A story written by each of the judges closes the anthology. This is so future To Hull And Back competition entrants can see the types of stories the judges write and learn about their tastes. I hope this might give writers a better chance of penning a successful story for future competitions.

I'd like to express my utmost thanks to all the authors of the stories that appear in the 2019 anthology. It's an honour to be able to present them in this collection.

Chris Fielden

CONTENTS

JUDGE'S STORIES

ACKNOWLEDGEMENTS

Thank you to Christie Cluett, John Holland, Mark Rutterford, Mel Ciavucco, Mike Scott Thomson, Steph Minns and Tom Parker for helping me judge the competition. John and Mike are both previous To Hull And Back competition winners. Myself, Christie, Mark, Mel, Steph and Tom belong to a writing group in Bristol called Stokes Croft Writers: www.christopherfielden.com/about/stokes-croft-writers-talking-tales.php

Thanks to David Whitlam for designing the cover of this book. You can learn more about Dave's artwork here: www.davidwhitlam.com

Thanks to David Fielden for building and maintaining my website. Without him, I'd never have created a platform that allowed the greatest writing prize in the known macrocosm to have been conceived and launched. You can learn more about Dave's website services at: www.bluetree.co.uk

And finally, a GARGANTUAN thank you to everyone who entered the To Hull And Back contest this year. The volume of entries has enabled me to increase the prize fund for the next competition for the sixth consecutive time. Without the support of all those who entered, this simply wouldn't be possible.

WINNING STORIES

CASSANDRA'S WEEK

The winning story, by Alan MacGlas

Kelsey Andrew discovered that he could see the future while watching the draw of the national lottery, alone in his flat on a Saturday evening, eating an apple doughnut. The apple doughnut wasn't great, but it was the nearest he could get to Manfred's strudel, made to Manfred's Austrian grandmother's recipe, which Manfred himself was no longer around to make.

Kelsey did not usually watch the lottery draw. He had found himself faced with a programme about the origins and locations of the Garden of Eden, featuring interviews with various loons who asserted a conspiracy by international powers to prevent discovery of the Tree of Knowledge. Kelsey was fairly sure that international powers were too preoccupied bribing one another and fixing posh schools for their children to worry about preventing discovery of anything except their extramarital affairs. So he switched TV channels before the loons could get into his brain, and landed on the lottery.

He *knew*, the moment the balls started whirling, that none of his numbers would be drawn. He really did. He didn't guess. He didn't calculate. He *knew*.

His knowledge went further: he saw that he would never win the lottery, even if he lived a hundred years.

He saw, too, that investing in lottery tickets was the only thing in his life that represented any kind of long-term planning.

He chewed his doughnut slowly, staring at the television screen. *You'd think,* he thought bitterly, *that this new enlightenment might reveal something useful, such as next week's winning lottery numbers.* It was small compensation that, instead, it showed him why such a thing was impossible.

He opened a bottle of wine, poured himself a large glass, watched *Match of the Day*, and went to bed.

*

The British Sunday presents no challenge to clairvoyance. It rained on and off. The wind blew.

*

Monday morning was when things began to become different. True, he sat on his usual train to work, with the usual people in their usual places around him. Such as that irritating woman who always occupied two seats, one each for her and her bag. The way her eye-liner turned up at the corners of her turned-down eyes. The chemical flare of her hair. Her lobster hands. Her knees.

But now he knew that her husband had left her three years ago, that she was still in daily hurt about it, and that she would never elicit the interest of another man – any man – to replace him.

Kelsey felt a surprising grief.

And the younger woman opposite. Going into marriage with desperate hope after an oppressed childhood and empty youth. She was really good at knitting novelty tea-cosies, but her husband would make her give it up, because he thought they were silly. Their shared bed would be cold within a year.

And again, the grief.

As for that boy in the rearmost seat... *No, please, Angel, no reading of your life: you are one of the few things that make this journey tolerable. The way your hair curls round your face. Your eyes. Your, to be frank, arse. Last Friday, you waited to let me off the train first, as if you didn't like my looking at it. Sorry, Angel, I'm only queer, you can kill me but please don't hate me.*

*

Oh joy. A committee meeting. He picked up his brief on the new accounting system. Last Friday, he hadn't understood any of it. Now he understood all of it. It was bollocks.

"It seems to me," said the Director, "that we'll have to run the old and new systems in parallel for *two* years, not one. Is that right, John?"

"That's very much the way I see it," concurred John, nose glutinously brown above his moustache.

"With respect—" began Kelsey, which was a lie.

"And that means," said the Director, "we're going to have to find more fat to cut from the budget. Again. Neil."

Neil's bald head shone with indignation. "We've been cutting fat from the budget for the last three years. Except it isn't fat any more, it's flesh. It's actual limbs."

"But we don't—" began Kelsey again.

"We need to get our ducks in a row," said the Director. "We've been round this buoy before. If we bite the bullet now, the proof of the pudding will emerge in due course."

"All you need," snapped Kelsey, "is to transfer Alia Iqbal from Human Resources. She knows the systems, she wants to work part-time, and she's brilliant. Problem sorted."

He was right. It was the best solution. But they looked at him as if he'd suggested they go to sit in the park because it was such a nice day.

"Well, we'd all like to live in that simple world, Kevin," said the Director, smiling fishily at him. "But it won't do. Will it, John?"

"I don't think it would work," agreed John, having not thought about it at all.

And, after the meeting, the Director would say privately to John, "I think young Kenneth is rather out of his depth. He goes off half-cocked with these half-baked ideas."

"Kes is good at what he does," John would reply unctuously, meaning that whatever Kelsey did wasn't important.

*

Tuesday. Getting lunch at his usual sandwich bar, Kelsey watched the young assistant as she prepared his chicken panini. Nice girl, as yet unspoiled by employment. She actually enjoyed being into her apron at half-seven every morning.

"Listen," said Kelsey, "the owner of this place owes a loan-shark, and he's going to do a runner in five weeks' time. You can get yourself a job with John Lewis if you apply tomorrow."

"You on commission?" she giggled, laying tomato slices.

"But next March—" began Kelsey.

"What?"

He stared at her having the most frenzied orgasms of her life with a new boyfriend next March. "Don't worry about it. Hold the mayonnaise."

*

Back in the office, he rang his big sister, Caroline.

"Hi, Cro."

"Hey, bro. How you doing?"

"Fancy eating this evening? It's on me."

"You won the lottery?"

"I'll never win the lottery. That's what I want to talk about."

They met in a pizza restaurant, ate pizza, and drank a modest quantity of modest red wine.

"So, Kes: what's happening?"

"I've had this weird experience."

"How weird?"

"It's like I can see the future. Suddenly, I seem to know everything."

"Like every other man on the planet."

"I mean it. I – I *understand* everything. It's like – walls falling down, fog clearing away, huge patterns coming into focus—"

She cut through this blether. "How's Manfred?"

"Dunno. Haven't seen him for weeks."

"You split with him?"

"We weren't really an item. We're better as friends."

"Kes."

"He's 10 years older. And he's not even my type."

"Who is your type?"

"We're going off the subject."

"What subject?"

"I told you. I can see the future."

"You been taking something?"

"No, I haven't. I mean, the occasional joint, but nothing unhealthy."

"If you can see the future, tell me what I'm going to have for dessert."

"It doesn't work like that," he protested.

"How does it work, then?"

"It doesn't *work* at all. It's just – how things are."

His sister eyed him sceptically, chewing mushroom and salami. "Kes, you need to get out more. Find a nice boy. Get laid. Have fun."

"Yeah. I should, actually."

"Hey, let me tell you. I met this guy. He works with Janine. We went dancing and…"

Kelsey was content to let her gossip. He did not tell

her that the guy she was telling him about was already married.

Neither did he tell her that she would have chocolate ice-cream for dessert, which she did. If he had told her, she would have changed her mind and had strawberry instead, which he also knew, and also didn't tell her.

*

On Wednesday, Kelsey arrived punctually at his office, looked through the papers stacked in his tray, and tipped them all into the waste-bin. Then he filtered some fresh coffee, put up his feet, read *Private Eye* and finished the crossword.

He exited the office before noon and walked to the city centre. People on the street waved their futures at him like a siege of sandwich-boards. He ignored them.

He slowed as he came to Oscar's. It had been a while since his last visit. But why not? He entered with the remembered prickle of possibility. *Hi guys, only looking, nothing dangerous or diseased.*

He recognised one man standing at the far end of the bar, with a cream moustache and pot belly, drinking lager from the bottle. They raised eyebrows in mutual greeting.

"Hey, Kes, how are you?" said the cream moustache.

"Fine. You?" Kelsey couldn't remember his name.

"Yeah, good." The man's gaze seemed attentive, but not for the usual reason. Something wary. This was explained by his next words: "Manny was saying he hasn't seen you for a while."

"Manfred?"

"Yeah. We're kind of together. Didn't you know?"

"No," said Kelsey. "I didn't know." But now he did.

"Manny said you weren't an item. Is that right?"

"Yeah. No. Just friends. No problem."

All the same, it hurt, that Manfred had found another guy already. It hurt to be less desirable than an older man with a cream moustache and a pot belly. Sharing cocks and kisses. Eating Manny's Granny's apple strudel.

He got the guy's name: Eric. Oh, with a K. OK. *Good to see you, Erik. Tell Manfred I said hello.*

*

Thursday. Kelsey strolled along to the Director's office and wafted the door open with his foot.

"Ah, Kevin. What did I want to see you for?" murmured the Director, squinting at his screen as though it bore clues to untold treasures.

"Nothing," said Kelsey. "I just came to tell you that you're going to give glandular fever to the girl in Ruislip who siphons your arse every month. She'll be off work for six weeks with no sick-pay and two kids to look after. If you were anything other than a complete knob-head you might care, but you're not, so you won't. Also, I'm resigning at the end of the month to spend more time with my penis. Have a nice day."

"Good, good," said the Director, still deep in his screen. "Keep me posted."

*

In the evening, Caroline rang him at home.

"You were right about that bastard," she said mournfully.

8

"What bastard?"

"I told you."

"Oh, right, Janine's friend. The guy you went dancing with. Why's he a bastard?"

"He's married is why."

"Aw, Cro, I'm sorry." He frowned. "How d'you mean, I was right? I didn't tell you anything about him."

"You said you could see the future. Well, you were right, he's a lying bastard."

Kelsey mentally scanned these words. No, a complete *non sequitur*. But make one comment about female logic and he was toast.

"How did you find out?"

"Janine told me. Why do I always fall for married bastards?" Now she sounded ready to weep.

"I don't suppose he meant to hurt you. He's just a dumb guy who wants his cock sucked on a regular basis like the rest of us."

"Then he needs a woman all mouth and no brain," said Caroline. "Oh, Kes. You're not a bastard. Why can't more men be like you?"

Because the population would die out, was why.

*

Friday. Kelsey rose at his usual hour, exercised, breakfasted, shat, shaved and showered as normal, and walked to the station in a red shirt over fawn trousers and his best moccasins. He did not step into anything unpleasant. *I, Kes Andrew, spruce and minty-breathed, well-educated, mild of temper, gay as a carnival and safe as an unopened packet of condoms, present myself for public intercourse.*

The morning was fine. The train ran on time.

When it drew into the terminus, he watched his fellow passengers debark and begin their matinal translation into office workers and interviewees and shoppers and slaves. He prepared to follow them along the platform.

"Excuse me."

He turned and found himself addressed by the Angel. Bright green eyes and soft hair and beautiful mouth.

"Excuse me. I – happened to see you Wednesday. Lunchtime. Er..." The Angel's words were blurred; there seemed to be a sort of beat in his throat. "Going into – er – Oscar's."

Kelsey saw, in the instant way one does, that the flight of commuters had left no one else near them, here on the platform. That the Angel had seen this as an opportunity. That the kid was being both brave and terrified.

"Yes?"

"I'm sorry. You don't know me at all. Tell me to push off if I'm – out of order..."

Something began to open in Kelsey's depths.

"No problem. Yeah, I was at Oscar's. It's a nice bar when it's quiet. I didn't notice you there."

"No – I was just passing, I've never been inside. I recognised you because – I've seen you on the train sometimes. I was wondering..."

Kelsey waited while the boy struggled, then prompted, "It's a gay pub. I mean, it's used by gay people. Like me."

"Oh, right." Relief. The green eyes emboldened. "As I say, I've never been inside, so I don't know – er..."

"It's like any other bar. Usual regulations. How old are you, if it's not a rude question?"

"20."

"So, old enough to buy a drink." They could both smile, and they both did. He had an angelic smile. One of the angels who didn't fall with Lucifer's legions, but perhaps watched them go rather wistfully.

"Well. I wondered..." The Angel drew a breath. "I wondered if I could meet you. There. Some time. For a drink."

O Sweet Lord. This was really happening. "Sure. I'd love to. Today?"

"Oh. No, I can't, today." Worried. "I'm sorry. Could you – tomorrow...?"

"Tomorrow's Saturday."

"Oh. Yeah." Beginning to panic. "Sorry. Well..."

Kelsey laughed. "Saturday's fine for me, if you can make it."

"Yeah, sure. What time would you like to...?"

"I'm easy. Shall we say, 12 o'clock? That'll give us plenty of time. For whatever."

"That'd be great."

*

There on the railway platform, for the first and last time, Kelsey Andrew looked into his own future. He saw himself in another 14 years, dying in the arms of this boy, wetted by his tears. Dying of an influenza virus that the boy himself would unwittingly pass into him.

But it would be the life of a great love. Love to death.

Or he could, here, now, reject it and live longer. Years and years longer.

There comes a time, at least once in every life, when Eden reveals itself to you. The only question then is whether you enter or whether you don't.

He ate of the fruit of the tree, and did not hesitate. "I'll look forward to it. See you tomorrow."

~

Alan MacGlas' Biography

A Londoner by birth and Glaswegian by accident, Alan MacGlas is a retired government servant and current professional editor of stories and poetry. He came to writing late in life, and has inflicted upon the world one book of miscellaneous articles, stories, poems and bagatelles *(The Collected Homework of Albert Gulliver Trumpshaw)* and one pamphlet of proper poetry *(Mortal Clay)*, neither of which is available from Amazon or any good booksellers.

Being an accomplished pianist and mildly autistic, he loves classical music, wine, mountains and out-of-season seaside towns. He detests poetry.

~

Alan MacGlas – Winner's Interview

1. What is the most interesting thing that's ever happened to you?

Regrettably, I have several candidate answers to this question that either fall under the Official Secrets Act or are too graphic for a general audience. When I was young and foolish, I did once decide that the best response I could make to a dozen National Front activists who were intimidating Saturday shoppers in

Lewisham High Street was to take one of their newspapers and tear it to pieces in front of them. Lively exchanges followed.

2. Who is the most inspirational person you've ever met and why?

Again there are several candidates, but I will mention particularly my late girlfriend, Caroline Grier Kerr. Her talent, perception, encouragement and early death inspired me to leave a career which had become a sterile cocoon and change my life completely. It is not too strong to say that I may well be alive today only because of her.

3. Which authors do you most admire and why?

Kathy Acker. She taught me what it means to be a writer without compromise. She took language apart and put it back in whatever way she needed to convey ideas and feelings that were otherwise inexpressible.

Anna Akhmatova. How she and her poetry survived at all between the death of Lenin (1924) and the death of Stalin (1953) is a matter of astonishment – many of her friends and their works didn't. Perhaps the poetry of Marina Tsvetaeva might be even more exquisite, that of Osip Mandelstam of greater breadth and human perception, and the literature of Boris Pasternak on a grander scale; but for icy integrity, personal truth, and beauty wrought from ruin and despair, Akhmatova stands with any poet in history.

Emily Brontë. I took *Wuthering Heights* with me to read during the evenings of a solitary camping trip in the Highlands. I thought it was the greatest novel I'd ever read, and although there are many great novels that I acknowledge and love, I've still never met one that exceeded it.

John le Carré. A great story-builder and literary craftsman. Not faultless, perhaps – his female characters are not always convincing, tending to form as foils to the male characters around them – but his books are always a wonderful read.

J P Donleavy. Rude, cynical, provocative, bitter, sometimes unexpectedly elegiac, but above all hilarious.

Don DeLillo. Stands with Roth and Updike as one of the literary pillars against whom all other US novelists have had to measure themselves in the past 50 years.

Joseph Conrad. A unique novelist, almost as splendidly isolated in English literature as Goya is in European art.

Frank Richards. His sheer output was incredible (literally so – it was famously doubted by George Orwell) but he wasn't just a hack writer of stories for boys. He created a world that was of its time, which is now dated – British public schools in the heyday of the British empire, governed by virtues and values that establishment Britons liked to think typical of themselves – but also timeless, sometimes beautiful, and always with its heart in the right place. He never patronised his youthful readers, most of whom would never even see the inside of a public school, and he taught them much good by stealth.

4. When and why did you start writing short stories?

I started writing short prose pieces – sometimes fact, sometimes fiction, sometimes unclassifiable – along with poems, about 10 years ago when I joined a Glasgow writing-group. This led to readings at poetry evenings and other literary events. Apparently I have quite good presence and projection when reading, and people are surprised when I tell them that in fact I'm extremely nervous (I have mild Asperger's, and can physically lock up under stress), but I do like the rapport and reaction with an audience when it goes well.

5. Where do your ideas and inspiration come from?

Although I have always been an accomplished prose writer and editor, I'm not naturally creative, and poor at plotting. I think the few short stories I have completed each stemmed from a single idea, perhaps little more than an image, round which they grew organically; but to be honest I don't remember much about the origins of any of my compositions. 'Cassandra's Week' is an example: I really can't remember where it came from; it may even have started life as a serious story. Anyway, writers and artists talking about their motives and processes are a bore. We should just do what we do and shut up about it.

6. Where do you write?

In my study. Yes, I have a study.

7. How do you cope when your writing is rejected?

Rejection without explanation isn't worth a reaction. Rejection with explanation is salutary – I've usually found myself agreeing with criticism, or at least finding it reasonable. But I haven't submitted many works yet, so my experience of failure is not much larger than my experience of success (which, to be clear, is small).

8. Who has published your work before?

No one. I have self-published a poetry pamphlet, distributed only to friends and family, whose duty it is to suffer.

9. Why did you choose to enter the To Hull And Back competition?

I was advised to enter by a friend and fellow contestant, who is now bitterly regretting her generosity.

10. What will you spend your prize money on?

Given that Windows 7 will no longer be supported by Microsoft from the end of this year and my sight isn't what it used to be, probably a new computer with a bigger screen.

11. What has been your proudest writing moment so far?

The registering of my poetry pamphlet with the British Library. Although I have edited many anthologies by other writers, this was the first which was entirely my own work and design. Even if I publish nothing else I shall still be happy to leave it as my personal testament.

12. What advice would you give to novice writers?

As an editor, the only general advice I ever give to

writers is: READ. Read a lot, and when you've done that, read a lot more. Years ago, the great pianist Sviatoslav Richter was judging a piano competition, and was observed to be marking the competitors either 20/20 or zero. When asked why, he replied, "Either they can play or they can't." It's the same with writing. If you can write, you will. If you can't, please don't. Or, at least, don't send it to me for editing. I can make bad writing less bad, and I can make good writing better, but I can't turn bad writing into good.

GERONIMO

The second place story, by Steve Sheppard

It's not every day you open your front door to find a giraffe in the porch.

Not actually in the porch, obviously. That would be absurd; a giraffe is, as you probably know, quite a tall animal, and certainly taller than my porch, which is, well, porch-sized.

To clarify then. The giraffe was standing outside the porch.

Leaving aside the conundrum of how it had managed to press the front door bell without possessing fingers to perform the task, I decided to concentrate on the bigger picture, as it were. The bigger picture being the fact that there was a giraffe standing in my front garden in Croydon.

All I could actually see of the beast from my current position of relative safety just inside the house were four legs. The body, neck and head of the giraffe were out of sight, hidden by the overhang of the porch.

You may well ask how, in that case, I could be sure that it was a giraffe at all.

Two reasons. First, the legs of a giraffe are unmistakable, both in terms of their length, or maybe that should be height, and their colouring. Also, these legs were quite thin. Very giraffy, in fact. They could not be mistaken for, say, the limbs of a camel or an especially tall zebra.

Second, I could hear a voice calling out. "Delivery of one giraffe, male, four years of age, to Mr Benjamin Sprockett." This appeared to confirm my hypothesis.

The voice seemed to be coming from somewhere over my head and was muffled by the intervening roof of the porch, but nevertheless the gist of what it was saying was quite clear. I debated briefly with myself whether a giraffe would have that clarity of tone but immediately dismissed the idea as fanciful, and so concluded that there was a second individual also in attendance, and that this second individual was, on the balance of probabilities, human.

I was reluctant to step outside and thus risk being crushed under the hooves of the massive creature, which could cause serious damage if their owner decided to undertake a bit of general trampling. And so, pulling the door to and securing it with its chain, which might or might not restrain a giraffe in full flight, I hurried upstairs to the bathroom, which overlooked the porch and front garden, and also enjoyed a magnificent view of the roof of the Ashcroft Theatre in the middle distance.

Kneeling on the toilet seat, I opened the bathroom window.

The head of the giraffe was still some distance above my own and appeared to be engaged in a long overdue cleaning of my gutter with its tongue.

However, perched somewhat precariously on the animal's back at my eye level was a small, rotund man with ginger hair, wearing an ill-fitting brown uniform which looked as if it may have been designed in the dark. With his right hand, he was holding firmly, even grimly, to a rope looped around the lower neck of the giraffe. In his left hand, he held a clipboard at which he squinted through a pair of wire-framed pince-nez as he saw me appear at the window.

"Excuse me," I called across to the man, who waved cheerily at me, almost dropping his clipboard in the process.

"Ah, hello, sir," he replied. "Do I have the honour of addressing Mr Benjamin Sprockett?"

I nodded.

"Excellent. If you would be good enough to sign here…" and he reached across with the clipboard. The gap, however, was too great and the clipboard ceased its journey a good five feet from the bathroom window. I did not consider this to be as great a calamity as the man on the giraffe clearly did. "Bother," he said, although bother was not the word he used. I forgave him the profanity in the circumstances.

"Sign for what?" I asked, although I entertained a deep suspicion that I already knew the answer.

"Why, for Geronimo, of course." He waved his left hand vaguely up and down a few times, nearly dropping the clipboard as he did so. I understood that he was indicating the giraffe, possibly thinking I had failed to notice the animal.

"Geronimo?" I ventured ingenuously.

"Yes, indeed," said the man, waving the clipboard again, but this time gripping it more tightly to prevent its escape.

"You mean this giraffe." I felt it was important to move the conversation on.

"Of course, Geronimo," explained my human visitor in the sort of way that suggested he believed all giraffes were named Geronimo.

"I didn't order a giraffe." This was a point that needed making, I decided.

"Yes, you did."

"No, I didn't."

"Well, yes, no you didn't, but it was of course implied." Whilst pleased that we were not about to engage in a lengthy, pointless bout of 'yes-you-did, no-I-didn't'-ing, I was unsure what he meant by the word 'implied'. So I asked.

"What do you mean – implied?"

"It was in the small print."

"I don't read small print."

"Well, no, of course not, who does?"

"Especially small print on forms that I have not looked at."

"As you can see," he continued, beginning to sound quite exasperated, "I am trying to get you to sign the form now, Mr…" and he referred to his clipboard, "Sprockett."

"Are you suggesting that I have somehow agreed to

take delivery of this giraffe despite not yet signing anything to confirm that?"

"No, I mean yes, that is to say, I mean, well, it's the introductory offer, isn't it?"

"Is it? What introductory offer?"

"Yes, it's in the small print."

"Which, as we have established, I haven't read."

Whilst I was more than happy for the giraffe to keep eating the sludge and other murky detritus out of my gutter, the morning was drawing on and I had other things which I could be doing. I wasn't sure what they were but undoubtedly something would occur to me before long.

However, I was mildly intrigued. "Who are you, exactly?"

"My name is Bob."

"Pleased to meet you, Bob," I said, not completely honestly. "However, that's not what I meant. Who do you represent? A company maybe? A zoo perhaps."

"Silly me, I should have said right from the outset. I'm from Animazon."

I thought I'd misheard. "Do you mean Amazon?"

Bob laughed. "Oh, no, not Amazon. I get asked that all the time. No, we are Animazon, much the same but we specialise, as you can see, in fauna," and again the clipboard waved up and down to indicate the giraffe.

"Including giraffes. I see, although I'm not sure that you can classify a giraffe as 'fauna', the dictionary definition of which is 'the animals of a particular region, habitat, or geological period'. Unless Croydon undergone some sort of massive geological transformation overnight, I don't think a giraffe could be accurately described as an animal native to this locality."

I had clearly confused my visitor, who looked at me with two deep lines of perplexity running down his forehead just north of both his nose and his pince-nez.

"Well, perhaps 'fauna' is the incorrect terminology. Animals would be better. The Animal Kingdom, as it were. All that passed through the doors of Noah's Ark are available on sale or return from us here at Animazon." He seemed happier again, having got that off his plump chest.

"So, nothing to do with Amazon then."

"Indeed not. Entirely separate company. Splendid though Amazon are for obtaining books and lampshades and so forth, you would be hard-pressed to obtain a giraffe at 48 hours' notice from them. Or indeed a wildebeest. Or..." I could see he was trying to think of some other type of creature; if his knowledge of the animal kingdom was restricted to just giraffes and wildebeests, it could be argued he was in the wrong job.

Meanwhile, the words 'sale or return' had caught my ear.

"Well, Bob," I said, summoning up a reluctant smile from somewhere deep inside. "As I did not order any giraffes in general, and specifically no giraffe named Geronimo, and as I have not signed to accept delivery, and as you have just mentioned that you operate a sale or return policy, I thank you for your time and this unexpected but interesting half hour, and I bid you good day. Please shut the gate after you. Or ask Geronimo to do it if you can't reach the latch."

I started to shuffle off the toilet seat but at that moment, Geronimo, who had obviously finished his dredging of my gutter and had heard his name mentioned, bent his neck and stuck his head through the bathroom window, taking extra sustenance in the form of a tube of toothpaste and a bar of Coal Tar soap as he did so. He fluttered his long lashes at me and smiled.

Well, it looked like a smile, but perhaps he was just feeling bilious from the sludge in the gutter, not to mention the toothpaste and soap.

At that point, the 'William Tell Overture' burst forth from inside the house. I recognised it as the ringtone on my mobile phone and it certainly caught the attention of Geronimo. He pushed his head fully into the bathroom, brushing past me as I stepped warily back against the wall. The giraffe's long neck twisted from side to side as he attempted to find the source of the music. His head reached the open door of the bathroom and, still smiling benignly, Geronimo peered out on to the landing where I had left my phone sitting on a side table.

Spotting the instrument, he stuck out his tongue, now mercifully clean of gunk from the gutter, and deftly transferred the phone from the table to his mouth, where he held it delicately between his floppy lips. Reversing his head back into the bathroom and turning it in my direction, Geronimo spotted me backed up against the tiling. His head approached me with the phone held in his mouth. *William Tell* was still merrily playing, although I was mildly surprised that the voicemail had not yet kicked in.

Geronimo dropped the instrument into my hand, which I had stretched out in an attempt to ward off the beast. He looked friendly enough, what with the smiling, but there could be only one loser in a coming together of giraffe, man and bathroom wall. Geronimo's head disappeared back out of the window and I held the phone to my ear.

"Hello?" I said in an understandably wavering voice.

My daughter, Amy, replied, "You took your time, Dad. Anyway, I'm just ringing to wish you happy birthday."

Happy birthday? Was it my birthday? I had quite forgotten.

"Erm, thank you, dear," I said, not willing to admit forgetting my own birthday in case it should prompt Amy to start thinking of the words 'home' and 'nursing'.

"Have you got the present I sent?"

"Present?"

"Yes. Hasn't it arrived? It should have been delivered at midday."

"Delivered?" It seemed I was only capable of repeating random words. I wasn't generating much coherent thought. Giraffes standing in one's front garden can have that effect.

"I knew you needed company and you don't like dogs, so I thought this would fit the bill. And you don't even have to take it for walks."

I stared stupidly at the phone in my hand for what seemed ages.

"Are you still there? Dad?"

"Er, yes, dear, sorry. Are you saying that you have arranged for an animal to be sent to me? As a birthday present?"

"Yes, that's exactly what I'm saying. And I had to take out a subscription to Animazon Prime as well, to make sure I got next day delivery, by 12 o'clock. And it's now gone half past. I'll be demanding my money back."

So Amy had decided that what I really needed as a 60th birthday present was a giraffe? I'd always thought she was the sensible one. She had been Head Girl at school, after all, and was now a successful solicitor. How could I tell her that I had absolutely no requirement for a 20-foot tall giraffe, and nowhere to keep it if I had? I didn't even have a garage.

"No, don't go complaining, Amy dear," I said. "Your present has been delivered. It's outside now in fact, with the man from Animazon."

"Outside? What's it doing outside? You need to bring it indoors. It'll catch its death of cold."

Amy knew the size of my house very well and must be aware that squeezing a fully-grown giraffe into it was an impossibility. Also, her assertion that it might die of cold seemed highly unlikely. Yes, of course giraffes are native to the warmer climes of Africa, but they seem to survive quite happily in British zoos so were probably able to adjust to variations in temperature.

"I doubt if I've actually got room for Geronimo," I said. "It's a lovely thought but I think I'm going to have to refuse the delivery. I'm terribly sorry."

"Geronimo? Who's Geronimo?"

"Geronimo's his name."

"What a ridiculous name for a gerbil."

I paused, moved over to the window and peered out. Geronimo was still there, having by now taken a liking to my rose bushes. Bob waved again when he saw me reappear. There was no doubt that Geronimo was a giraffe. Not a gerbil.

I put the phone to my ear again. "Gerbil?" I asked carefully. "Not giraffe?"

"Giraffe? What on earth are you talking about, Dad? Why would I send you a giraffe? Do you think I'm made of money?"

I was a little concerned that the expense was the principal reason Amy had not ordered me a giraffe, but let it go. "I'll call you back," I said, and hung up.

I called to Bob. "I think there's been some mistake. That was my daughter, Amy, on the phone and she insists she ordered a gerbil." And just in case I had not made myself clear, "Not a giraffe."

Bob looked down at his clipboard and pursed his lips. "Dearie me," he said. "Would that be Mrs Amy Wotherspoon?"

"That's her."

"It was Mrs Wotherspoon who ordered the giraffe."

"No, she ordered a gerbil."

"Gerbil? Are you sure? Let me see," and Bob ran his finger down his clipboard. "Galapagos penguin, gecko, gerbil, giraffe... Ah, yes, I see what's happened. My colleagues in Dispatch have ticked the wrong animal. Easy mistake to make."

It seemed like a fairly fundamental mistake to me. "So you'll take Geronimo away?"

"Of course, sir. Sorry for the inconvenience."

"And bring a gerbil? By tomorrow perhaps, as my daughter has paid for Animazon Prime?"

"Oh dear, no, I'm afraid we're completely out of gerbils."

"I see. Very popular, are they?"

"Oh, no, it's not that," said Bob, frowning. "It's just that the lion has eaten them all."

~

Steve Sheppard's Biography

My first novel, *A Very Important Teapot*, which I like to describe as a comedy thriller, is due to be published by Claret Press this autumn and I am currently working on a sequel in the certain knowledge that many, many people will be clamouring for such a book once they read *Teapot*. Or not, but it's always good to be prepared.

Apart from half a dozen poems published in an anthology back when the world was in black and white, *Teapot* will be the first thing with my name intrinsically involved sitting on a bookshelf.

I was born and spent my formative and early adult years in the middle of the Surrey stockbroker belt but, having failed to meet any stockbrokers, I moved to rural west Oxfordshire over 20 years ago, where I live in the poorer part of an expensive and attractive not-quite-Cotswold village with my wife, a son who refuses to move out, and the latest in a series of tired cats.

I am now starting to wind down following a life spent working variously as a salesman, local government pen-pusher, prison officer, bingo manager and presently, as I reach my mellow years, something I'm not quite sure about in digital advertising within the motor trade.

RISE ABOVE IT

The third place story, by Kiare Ladner

I'd just taken a swig from the apple juice in my mother's fridge when the phone in her kitchen rang. I was tired, I was distracted; I put the receiver to my ear before registering what was in my mouth. While I gagged loudly in the sink, two voices competed for my attention. My mother's, unrestrained by her being dead, won out.

"Oh, Melody," she said, "stop being dramatic. It's not like you've never ingested bodily fluids from me before."

To suppress my annoyance at her, I turned up the volume on the phone.

"Hello?" said the refined, elderly male voice, now coming clearly down the line. "Am I speaking to Melody, Padma's daughter?"

"I'm Melody, and a daughter – but my mother's name was Pat."

"'Always charmed by a touch of reinvention," said the voice.

"Well, I don't know if you've heard," I said, "but my mother's time for reinvention has ceased."

"That's why I phoned. To offer sincere condolences—"

"Sincerely received. Though I didn't catch your name—?"

"Shankar," said the voice.

Shankar? My mother hadn't ever mentioned a Shankar.

"It means 'giver of bliss'," said Shankar. "Not a reinvented name, though I couldn't have chosen better myself."

"Ha, I wouldn't have chosen Melody in a million years. My mother wanted to call me Rhapsody but my father held her back."

"Your mother was a Great Character." Shankar gave a tinkling laugh. "Her energy was unique. It was my honour to be her yoga instructor."

"Oh," I said, "I see."

Though I didn't see at all. The image of my mother doing yoga was too peculiar. She'd been a stiff-jointed, tent-shaped person, not in the least physically inclined.

"We're dedicating our Tuesday practice to your mum," said Shankar. "Since you're in town, we wanted to invite you to come along."

Although built less like a tent and more like a brick, I was my mother's child when it came to physical agility.

"Me and yoga," I said, "hmm, not sure."

"Our practice is different to what you'd expect," said Shankar. "A variation on the tradition, adapted to what our attendees can do. The average age of the class is 74."

"I'm 47," I said, in hope that my relative youth would put him off.

"A spring chicken," he replied, before adding with a smile behind his cryptic words, "we will treat you kindly."

*

Clearing out my mother's flat, I heard her voice a lot. As well as my misery at losing her, I'd recently lost my job; without children or a partner, the years seemed to slope ahead pointlessly. My departed mother, however, was full of bolstering advice: "You have everything going for you. Don't be so negative. Rise above it, Melody, rise above." She boosted it with suggestions, such as: "Drinking urine is wonderful for the complexion. Stir your saucepan in the infinity sign to prevent burning. Have you ever considered applying to be an astronaut?" Yet, the more my mother cheered me on, the more curious I became about the single topic on which she kept schtum: Shankar and his yoga.

So it was that the following Tuesday I found myself outside The Studio in the woods on the hills of Aberystwyth. If I'd climbed to the venue with some trepidation, while we waited for Shankar, it was dispelled; my mother's age of 70 had evidently been bringing the average right down. Three students, with a similar number of stray hairs on their heads as on their chins, looked as old as god and as genderless. They introduced themselves as siblings rather than brothers or sisters: Bryn, Gwyn and Morgan.

Next to them on the stone wall, swinging plumply dimpled legs like a five-year-old, was a talkative woman called Angelika. "I've been in this town 79 years," she said. "Doing yoga for 78. Not in this studio which, as you can see, is quite recent. Designed in the late 60s in honour of Swami Sivananda."

Beside Angelika stood a wisp of a man with smoker's yellow fingers. He persisted in whistling through his teeth despite her frequent interruptions of, "Gilbert, hush."

Wanda, of spiky white hair and startlingly violet eyes, used one of the interruptions to mention my mother. "Padma joined us only last spring," she said. "From the start, she brought to the practice an aura of peace."

As I considered rearranging my genetically stiff demeanour to 'daughter of woman with aura of peace' – an identity I'd not had reason to explore before – Bryn, Gwyn and Morgan nodded in agreement.

I was saved having to attempt an ingenuous reply by Shankar's arrival. When he took my hands in his warm, dry embrace, my mother's voice flitted lightly into my mind's ear. "Isn't he a *beautiful* man?"

And, despite his being a good few years my mother's senior, despite my mother's and my taste in men differing significantly – with his dark wishbone limbs, his fine features, his silver ponytail and his luminescent eyes – for once, I had to agree.

*

The Studio was wood and glass with eight yoga mats set out on the floor. I waited until seven were taken. Shankar pointed to the last, "Your mother's," which I'd deduced, though it would hardly have been my instinctive choice. My mother was a front and centre type of person, whereas this mat was in the far corner by the back wall.

The class opened with a simple dedication to 'our dear friend, Padma, Melody's Mum' before Shankar led us into sun salutations.

The yogis went through the motions with a musical range of creaks and cracks. But the shapes they made... Despite the cabin having no mirrors, in warrior two I reckoned I was the only warrior-like one among them. As we melted into humble warrior, I told myself: smug as I felt, I should take care to appear humbly superior.

After we took a child's pose to rest, Shankar suggested sliding forwards into pigeon. While you'd imagine pigeon to be as ordinary as the bird, it isn't. One leg is stretched behind you, with the other folded in front, your shin at a right angle to your thigh. I struggled to make anything remotely resembling Shankar's split but, to my astonishment, the regulars took their versions without complaint.

From pigeon, we moved up in the bird world to crow. This involved squatting with palms on the ground and leaning forward onto elbows until legs lifted off. Wonky as they seemed, everyone achieved the balance – except me, who fell into a heap. Embarrassed, I laughed; Gilbert, then Bryn, Gwyn and Morgan, still upside down, joined in. As Wanda, Angelika and Shankar started laughing too, I noticed that the sound filling the room was amazingly squawk-like.

Perhaps heedful of the bird that couldn't hack it, Shankar prefaced the next pose with, *If it is available to you today,* before instructing, "Put the left shoulder under the left thigh."

I expected more hilarity as everyone collapsed. But that wasn't the case; all left shoulders except mine were under left thighs.

"Straighten the left arm," said Shankar. "Then the right."

14 arms spread out like aeroplane wings.

"Now," Shankar said, "lift the left foot lightly off the ground."

Everyone followed his instruction to balance solely on the balls of their right feet.

"And now," Shankar said, "lift the right."

I frowned. Had I heard correctly?

"If it is available to you today," Shankar continued, "then hover. And for those of you who want to take it further still... have a little fly."

Notwithstanding their wobbles, one by one, the yogis' right feet left the ground. And then, with it apparently being available to *all* of them today, they began to fly around the room.

"Take a rest in child's pose," Shankar said to me, as Gilbert flapped above my head. "Unless you'd like me to give you a hand?"

"Yes, *please*," I said, FOMO transcending any distant sense of pride.

Positioning us thigh to thigh, Shankar told me to relinquish my weight, to lean my heft into him. Then, slowly, he took me through the instructions until I was hovering two feet in the air. I could hear his breath, feel the smooth heat of his skin. "Did my mother do this?"

"Yes."

"Fly? By herself?"

"Yes," said Shankar. "But remember, she was older than you."

I was puzzling over what he had said, when out of nowhere, Angelika zoomed lopsidedly towards me. Next thing I knew, I'd taken off. While my body headed for the open window at the top of the room, Shankar shouted, "Don't fly out."

And I didn't but – for a moment – I felt as though I could. As though without it being any big deal, I could be on the other side of the glass, then in the forest, then above the town, soaring over the bay, the castle, the old college, the coloured seafront terraces, the little yellow flat with the seashell garden where my mother had lived. And then going further, I could follow the rail tracks through the countryside all the way back to London where my life for so many years had been lived hemmed in by anxiety and self-doubt and sense of obligation – to what, to what?

With my confidence in freefall, I came crashing to the ground.

"Oh, Melody," my mother sighed, "we've all got life issues. Rise above it."

*

When we lay flat on our backs in Shavasana, corpse pose, I thought of my mother's corpse. How she'd looked both like and not like herself, as if modelled in wax by a sculptor capable of imitating physical traits but lacking the artistry to capture more.

And now her *more*, whatever it was, was gone. While I could bring to mind the kinds of things she'd say, without her being alive, they lacked expansiveness. She could not change; I could not change for her. A future in which she changed, and I changed, and we had an altogether different relationship had passed.

And yet, that was not the whole of it...

Branches knobbled with buds swayed beyond the open window; light and shadow played alternately on the lids of my eyes. My mother's story didn't fit neatly together. She was *more* than the person I had known. She'd had facets that were not available to me to see. Such as the capacity to become a person who flew and found peace and in her last months knew a beautiful man who addressed her as Padma.

"Come back into yourselves," Shankar said. "Wiggle your finger and toes. When you are ready, come back into the room."

*

We closed the session with three Om's in a seated position. Hands at heart centres, heads bowed, we said, "Namaskar, Namaskar."

Afterwards, we squirted tea tree oil on our mats. While I was wiping mine down with a cloth, Shankar came over to me. I wanted to thank him but thanks didn't seem right. He laid his hand on my head with his thumb on my third eye. "We've done a lot of inversions today," he said, "so you may feel a bit high."

Never mind high, with his hand there I felt anointed. The moment he took it away, I slipped on my jacket and boots. I went to the door; I opened it. As spring's chill hit my cheeks, I knew my mother was the person I'd wanted to rush off to tell. Then, I thought how she'd kept this to herself, and a more complex feeling replaced my sorrow. But before I left The Studio, my perspective tilted once more.

"D'you enjoy it?" Gilbert called after me.

"Yes," I said. "Very much."

"Join us tomorrow, then," he said

"Same again?" I said. "More flying?"

"No," he said. "Tomorrow's the *advanced* class."

In memory of my mother, who never (to my knowledge) did yoga.

~

Kiare Ladner's Biography

As a child, Kiare Ladner wanted to live on a farm, run an orphanage and be on stage. As an adult, she found herself working for academics, with prisoners and on nightshifts.

Her short stories have been published in anthologies, broadcast on the radio and shortlisted in competitions, including the BBC National Short Story Award 2018. *Nightshift*, her debut novel, will be published by Picador in 2020.

HIGHLY COMMENDED STORIES

BREATHLESS

Highly commended story, by Eddie Mitra

Sunday, 22nd of May – I

I was never going to turn out OK. Looking back at my life, I realise I stood no chance against the wave of fuckedupedness that marked my psychosexual development.

My earliest memory of the female anatomy is my mother's naked body as she was stepping out of the shower while I, a mere boy of 10, was peeping through the open door in awe of the hairy lack between her legs. My earliest memory of being aroused was of her discovering me and spanking me on my bare bottom while calling me a 'naughty little pervert' without bothering to put on clothes. How about that?

Four years later, I would pay Dominika, my babysitter, £50 to let me finger her while my rich mother entertained various men at various restaurants of various hotels. But more on Mother later. I had my sexual awakening at 14, when I realised that I was paying top price for mediocre fingering of a mediocre pussy and I decided to upgrade.

Her name was Giovanna, an Italian prostitute who had no problem fucking kids if they had money and at least *some* facial hair, and I had plenty of both. I was a cunt-crazy kid who grew into a cunt-crazy teenager and now here I am, a man in his 30s who cannot – and will not – stop asphyxiwanking. You, decent people reading this, might know it better as autoerotic asphyxiation, but that's just a fancy name for a filthy thing and I think we've already established that I'm pretty fucking far from decent.

Monday, 23rd of May – Lisa

Lisa, the tall, smart and beautiful nymphet who was the answer to all my sexual prayers, left me exactly seven Mondays ago. After wallowing in self-pity and traipsing around my flat for a week, looking for glimmers of anything and not finding any, I reached the conclusion that a great orgasm was worth more to me than my life. So, why not? The risk of dying cock-in-hand, blue-faced and with my ex-girlfriend's knickers up my nostrils seemed to be a fair trade-off for the constant doublethink that I want to die because she left me and I want to live because she's not worth it.

So, for the sake of simplicity, I decided to leave this matter to chance by cutting off my oxygen supply while I rubbed it out to thoughts of naked women doing 'oh, for fuck's sake' things. I figured there was about a 50% chance that I would get my happy ending. As far as the other 50% goes, I dare you to name a better way of leaving this world than via the orgasm that quite literally took your breath away. So, in the very likely event that I have gone while coming, this journal should read as an overly detailed suicide note. Unless it happens tonight.

Tuesday, 24th of May – Mother

It didn't. So, Mother. My mother's obscenely rich. She was the sole heiress to the Faraday fortune, so honest work was a foreign concept to her. But to give herself the illusion of purpose, she started the Faraday Foundation to try and fix Africa. She kept busy by throwing charity dinner parties where rich people ate swordfish steaks, drank Armand de Brignac by the bucketful and patted themselves on the back for saving the poor and the hungry. How noble. Meanwhile, I was doing real charity work by giving money to a Polish immigrant in exchange for finger access to her vaginal canal. Truly noble.

Mother hated Lisa. But then again, Mother hated most people. "She's tall, smart and beautiful and you're a fat midget with a trust fund. Please tell me I didn't raise a fucking idiot," was my loving mother's verdict on my relationship.

Lisa loathed Mother, simply because Mother was so

easy to loathe. Mean, rude and controlling were just a few ingredients in this bitter cocktail named Fay Faraday that was so unpalatable to any outsider, or insider. At least outsiders had the luxury of leaving. Don't get me wrong, I didn't hate Mother, but I didn't exactly love her either. I felt that if she died, I could probably get myself to love her memory.

And, of course, as I expected, about a month into our relationship, she forced me to choose between her – money, house, slavery – and Lisa – love, sex, sometimes anal. She was tall, smart and beautiful and I was a fat midget with a trust fund. I obviously chose anal Lisa. Save for this card on my birthday:

33 years ago, I was in labour for 28 hours. I thought that would be the worst pain I would ever experience. Little did I know...

Happy birthday, James

I barely heard from Mother. But that didn't matter to me one bit as Lisa was more than enough and the great sex made up for the lack of money. While it lasted...

From once a day to twice a week to once a week to twice a month to never was the sexual countdown to the end of our relationship. Eventually, I was left with no girlfriend, no money and no real reason to live, which for Mother meant hitting the charity motherlode.

She set me up with *her* therapist and life-long friend, Dr Michael Gilbert, and all was paid for, of course, by the Faraday Foundation. I unequivocally declined, knowing full well that, due to my mother's manipulative nature, anything I would say to Dr Gilbert, she would eventually find out. *But*, low on funds and will to live, I am still ashamed at how quickly I caved when money changed hands. She had unknowingly agreed to sponsor my asphyxiwanking race with death on the condition that she play the part of the messianic mother. And I can find the fun in anything.

Wednesday, 25th of May – Dr Gilbert

Today, I'm having my fifth therapy session with Dr Gilbert. Dr Gilbert has been the only constant male presence in both my and Mother's lives. And before you get any dirty ideas, their relationship has never gone past demanding rich widow, gelded male companion. He's the moral equivalent of a windsock and acts as her outsourced conscience, justifying and enabling her actions with all the authority of a matchbox's echo.

"I completely agree, Fay," is his catchphrase. Hell, if she farted, he'd probably agree.

He's also 65 years old and more sexually repressed than an impotent catholic priest in Neverland. And, my god, the past five weeks have been the most fun I've ever had. Seeing that old fella squirm, sweat and stutter while I tell him, for example, that my orgasms were so intense, I couldn't even reach for the tissues.

"Have you ever tried wiping cum out of a rug, Dr Gilbert?" I asked him, as if I didn't know the answer already.

"No, James, I can't say that I have." He shifted uncomfortably in his chair.

"It's pointless. I had to throw the bloody thing away – it was like a Ritz cracker by the end."

For one hour every week, Dr Michael Gilbert is the unwilling one-man audience to my unabashed one-man show, *James Faraday: The Hanging Masturbator* and he's obviously not enjoying it. Unfortunately, Dr Gilbert, *I am*. In fact, I'm loving it and, in the words of the late

Freddie Mercury, 'The Show Must Go On'.

But, what really rocks my boat is the thought of him having to re-tell my adventures to Mother. "Well, Fay, I don't know how to say this, but sometimes, while he masturbates, you pop into his mind."

That, my friend, is a sensory nonpareil. I touch myself thinking of that shit. I really am pretty fucking far from decent.

Thursday, 26th of May – Sodomythical

Apparently, the male G-spot is 2 inches up the rectum, which means homosexuality might just be more natural than Anne Widdicombe believes. Whilst being gay might not be a choice, having great orgasms *is* and I've got nothing to lose. So, if I hoist the belt to the doorknob at just the right height, and I stick one of those suction dart dildos to the floor where my arse lands, I can stimulate my prostate while I asphyxiwank myself into an early grave.

This is a list of things I previously described as orgasmic: scratching an itch with a fart, lasagne, proving Mother wrong, orgasms. Put them all together and add the best sex you've ever had and you're not even close to what I managed to achieve here. This is a mechanism for complete hedonistic euphoria, a nirvana of decadence that transcends the material world – it's *sodomythical.*

I came so fucking hard today, I started weeping. I called Dr Gilbert right after and told him the whole story.

"I told you before, James, write it down and tell me in our session, OK? You don't need to call me every time something like this happens."

Oh no, Dr Gilbert, I really do. I think he's trying to limit our interactions.

Friday, 27th of May – Greyout/Blackout

When it comes to breath play, a greyout is what you're after. If your vision starts to blur, your lips start to tingle and your erection could give someone a serious concussion, you're in the sweet spot, my friend, you have about 20 seconds to reach your destination. Anything beyond that and you won't even know whether you're coming or going; anything beyond that is a blackout.

The difference between a greyout and a blackout is the same as between swimming and drowning: one second you're weightless, floating comfortably and giving yourself away to the waves and then, *swoosh*, out of nowhere, a titanic wave comes crashing down, you lose all control and the darkness envelops you. You then find yourself desperately gasping for air that never comes. And then it gets dark. Dark and quiet.

Today, I experienced my first blackout. Normally, your first and last blackouts are the same one, but I guess I got 'lucky' this time. I must have been unconscious for a while, because when I came to, a white crusty layer of dried saliva glazed my cheek.

For those few minutes while I was out, everything faded to black. There was no Lisa, no Mother and no pain. Nothing. As I got up and stood in front of the bathroom mirror, scraping the dried spit off my numbed face, I stared at myself and realised with stupor that it was still *me* looking back. I expected that returning from the dead would change me in some significant way or, at the very least, urge me to start a religion. *But,* I was surprisingly content – I had a taste of death and it tasted fine.

I called Dr Gilbert. He didn't answer, so I left a voicemail. I'm now certain he's trying to limit our interactions.

Saturday, 28th of May – When Sleep Finally Visits You

I spent the majority of last night staring stupidly at the ceiling where my mind was projecting cuckolding sex scenes of Lisa and that fella she started seeing worryingly fast after leaving me. He's one of those bodybuilder/life coach types, with a fully shaved body and a 'V' poking out of his trousers. The only thing *I* have poking out of my trousers, is un-tamed pubic hair that unfurls onto my gut and chest like a wildlife crossing on the motorway. He might be better looking, but I can make a mean cuppa that Lisa once described as 'better than sex'. In retrospect, she might have just meant better than sex with *me*.

It was early morning when sleep finally visited me, only to be violently disturbed by my phone ringing. I remember thinking, *Who the fuck still calls people? Sociopaths and the elderly, that's who.* So, I tried to ignore it – I was in no mood for any sociopathic old people that early in the day and in such a sleepy stupor. But the damned thing wouldn't stop ringing.

I eventually answered with discernible irritation in my tone. It was Annie, Dr Gilbert's assistant. In her characteristic languid, simpleton voice, she informed me that Dr Gilbert would not be able to see me anymore. I couldn't believe it. It looked like Dr Gilbert had finally retrieved his manhood from my mother's cold, manipulative clutches and took a decision against her will. Although I was somewhat proud, I couldn't just give up on the fun of torturing the old bastard.

"Did he give you a reason? Does Mother know?"

"Oh, no, darling, you don't understand. It's not that Dr Gilbert *won't* see you, it's that he *can't* see you. He's dead, James. Dead. He hung himself with his belt last night, in his office. Emma, his daughter, found him this morning. He was supposed to go for dinner at her house last night, but he didn't show, and he wouldn't answer her calls either. So, she got worried and, after checking his house, she came to the office and there he was, blue in the face, with a belt around his neck and, on top of everything, stark naked. Poor girl. He killed himself, James."

Sunday, 29th of May – Mother and I

I had dinner with Mother this evening, but she barely talked or even looked at me. It was mostly long stretches of chewing in silence, interrupted by my unsuccessful attempts to converse. Dr Gilbert's passing was clearly hanging in the air and she was being curt for a reason.

I couldn't help wondering whether she was being distant because she blamed me, or because she was afraid I would go the same way. I couldn't have possibly asked – she might have just wanted some passive companionship in a time of grief, and I'm clearly not the right person to pass judgment on how people choose to deal with loss.

But, as it turns out, my id and my cock have no such manners as all I could think of was a particular belt around a particular neck and, immediately, my erection started lifting the table off the floor as if this were a séance and whore ghosts were trying to contact the living for a shag. So, I hoovered up my fish, I said my goodbyes and got up to leave before dessert.

"The funeral's tomorrow at 12pm. I shall send Miles to pick you up."

"All right, Mother," I answered as I stepped out of the house and into the rainy city, chasing a release.

With one foot inside the house, I had already loosened my belt and, before I had even taken off my shoes, I was already buckling it around my neck. A minute later, out of breath, I released the champagne of victory. I popped this cork to quench my own thirst, but I shall finish the bottle in Dr Gilbert's honour, who never got to finish his. 'Til tomorrow.

~

Eddie Mitra's Biography

I'm 26 and I'm an aspiring writer/director with a few short films and short stories under my belt. My writing generally explores the uncomfortable, the unconscious and the various things people feel that society has deemed unacceptable. I treat themes such as death, addiction or sexual deviancy with humour and irreverence because I find people who take life too seriously are helplessly boring and annoying.

My greatest fear is that writing is therapy and that someday I will be healed.

EXHIBIT: WOMAN AND BIRD

Highly commended story, by Karen Jones

The little bird on Minerva's hat tells her things. At the cinema, he tells her this is the day and the man is the one. Minerva isn't like other matinee attendees. She doesn't crinkle-crankle sandwiches from tinfoil, doesn't sip-slurp tea from a recyclable cup. She sucks seeds from a packet she shares with the bird on her hat. The hat that sits atop her wig.

She senses Bird's claws dig deeper, almost through her hat to her wig, shifting her chignon, knows he's ready to squeal and straighten out his wings. She shakes the seed bag to distract him, but he will not be distracted. And there it is. The sound of the man's rump assaulting the too-small chair. His big hands ripping open his bag of crunchy sweets. She feels his breath on her neck.

"You're in my seat, old witch. In my seat. Always in my seat." His voice sends a rumble through her head that makes Bird tremble.

She hears Bird squawk, "In-my-seat-in-my-seat-in-my-seat," then screech his laugh.

She gives Bird more seeds to hush him, creaks round and looks at the man from her one eye. She smiles her empty mouthed smile, holds out her four-fingered right hand and says, "We've never been formally introduced. I'm Minerva." The sound of her own voice in public surprises her. Softer, scratchier, weaker than she remembers.

"Oh, you're bothering to answer me today, eh? Well you're in my seat," the bulk blusters. "My seat. Always been my seat. You're in my seat."

Minerva sighs, shakes her head. "One can sit anywhere. I like this seat. And, more importantly, Bird likes this seat, that's why he's the one who usually deals with you."

The man snorts. "What? That thing in your hat that you keep covering in seeds? How could that deal with me? And by the way, you should take the hat off – it blocks my view."

Minerva wags a finger at him. "Do not refer to Bird as a 'thing' and do not pretend you and he haven't interacted. Anyway, if it really troubles you, you could always arrive earlier than us to claim 'your' seat. Ah, but you do, don't you? Bird has seen you skulk around outside, waiting for us to pass. Bird knows your kind.

Bird sees. Bird knows how lonely you are."

The redness of the man's face illuminates the darkness. He jabs a fat finger at the chair. "You're in my seat. That's my seat and you're in it."

Minerva reaches out to pat his hand, but he recoils, protecting his sweets as though she might try to steal one. She smiles. "Bird thinks we should watch the film together then you can follow us home, have some tea and some conversation. It's a while since I spoke to anyone. Bird thinks I need to speak more, thinks it's the same for you. What do you say?" When she cocks her head, her hair and hat and Bird slide to one side.

The man's face is a mixture of confusion, hatred and sadness. "My seat," he mumbles, before shrinking back into the chair as far as his and its frame allow.

When the film is over, Minerva gathers her belongings into her threadbare bag-for-life and picks up her walking stick. She hirples out of the cinema, Bird on her head facing the man who follows them 10 paces behind. When she reaches her front door, she turns to find the man standing at the gate, examining his shoes. His big tweed jacket strains at the arms and its weight has made him sweat. He wipes his glistening head with a white handkerchief.

"Come," Minerva says. "I'd like you to learn more about me. I think you may be the one to help. But first, tea. And perhaps some cake?"

His eyes widen at the mention of cake and he hurries up the path and into the hallway. He doesn't look as horrified at the mess in her house as people often do. The stacked newspapers always on the brink of collapse, the empty cans and bottles strewn across every surface don't seem to bother him at all. Minerva takes this as a good sign. Until they reach the kitchen and he sees the jars on the display shelf, moves closer, then reels back on his heels, steadying himself with one hand on the greasy cooker.

"Is that your eye? I mean, have you...?" He clasps his hand over his open mouth.

Minerva nods, a sharp nod that causes her hair to shift so suddenly it unsettles Bird who falls to the floor. She picks him up and perches him on an empty jar labelled 'heart'. "Yes, that's my eye. And next to it is my hair, and next to that my teeth. We'll talk about the others while I make the tea. I can't manage much food now – just some soup and the occasional seeds to suck – but I do enjoy my tea and I find visitors benefit from the strong, sweet kind."

He lets go of the cooker, rubs his hand on his jacket, then takes a seat with his back to the display.

She sets the kettle to boil on the hob. "Perhaps you could tell me your name? If we are to be friends, I should surely know your name?"

He coughs, finds his shoes fascinating again, and mumbles, "Francis."

"Well, Francis, here's the thing – it all started with toenails, as so many things do, don't you think?" She smiles at him, as though this will be common ground. "I just couldn't let them go, couldn't bear to think of someone else gathering them up, touching them, using them."

"Using them? For what?" he asks.

"Oh, well, you know how it was back then, the things we thought would be possible in the future that is today. I suppose I worried about being cloned and my double being used in crimes that I would have to pay for. I'm sure we all had those worries. And, of course, it turns out that it's perfectly possible now. They've cloned dinosaurs, after all. You and I have seen how that turned out."

His brow furrows. "But that's just a film. It's not..." He looks over his shoulder at the bird on the jar, takes a deep breath, sighs and nods. "But toenails are one thing – they have to be cut on a regular basis. What about the eye and the other... things?"

Minerva shrugs. "After the nails it was the hair. I didn't like leaving bits of myself all over the place, so I shaved it off, bought some wigs. It makes life easier, and I do enjoy the ritual of a razor. There are many hair containers in the attic. The one you see here contains the first shearing. Next, I had my appendix out – not through choice, I hasten to add – and asked if I could keep it. I had to pay, of course – it's really not the done thing, handing out organs, even to the original owner – but my husband left me more than well-off, so money has never been a problem."

Francis drums his fingers on the table. "But your eye..."

She laughs. The kettle screeches its readiness. "You're so obsessed with the eye. Yes, it was always trying to see the other eye. It was annoying. I had to pay a doctor abroad to have that removed, given that there was, in his opinion, nothing wrong with it. He has proved worth his weight in forints over the past few years as I downsize my body and place it where I can enjoy it."

She watches him examine her head to toe as she makes the tea and brings it to the table with the cake.

He ticks off on his fingers, "Nails, hair, appendix, eye, finger," – she waves her four-fingered hand at him – "there's more, isn't there?"

She pours the tea. "Pinky toe, spleen, one lung, one

kidney, half a liver – though the pesky thing grows back, I'm told. I'm half tempted to ask for a refund. Part of the bowel, part of the stomach. Anything I can do without goes in the jars. I can see myself as a woman of many parts rather than just this solid, lumpen thing."

She offers him cake. He accepts, choosing the largest piece and stuffing it into his mouth in one go.

She smiles. "You don't have to rush it – it's all for you. As I say, I can't really eat, since the..."

"Stomach and bowel being in jars," he says, spraying her with cake crumbs.

She claps her hands. "*Exactly.* You can have a look at them if you like."

He shakes his head so violently she can hear his jowls flap. "Sorry about the crumbs. I'm always doing that. My wife used to hate it."

"Not to worry." Minerva gathers the crumbs into her skirt and tips them into a saucer. "Bird and I shall enjoy them later. So, you're married?"

"Was. I got fat. She didn't like it. Left me."

Minerva pats his hand. "And is that why you're so angry all the time?"

His only answer is a deep, thick sniff.

Minerva fixes Bird into her hair, gets up and gathers the plates. "So now that we're friends, do you think you can help me?"

He raises his eyebrows. "Oh, well, maybe. What do you need? I could help with your shopping. That would be nice. I could stop in for some cake and a chat now and then."

Minerva laughs. "Heavens, no. Nothing like that, lovely though it's been. And we could continue to do that afterwards, if you like. No, you see I haven't managed to convince anyone to remove my heart yet and that is the real goal. It's what it's all been leading up to." She picks up a knife. "So, I wondered, if you wouldn't mind. I'll pay you, of course, more than I paid the Hungarian for all the other minimising."

His eyes bulge, he grips the table and stares at her. Then he laughs. "Oh, I thought you were being serious just then. *Ha.* Good one."

Minerva leans across the table and clasps his hand. "Oh, but I am, my dear. And you did say you'd like to help."

"But without your heart… I mean… no. It's not possible. If even a trained surgeon, albeit a clearly dodgy one, wouldn't do it, how could I? You can't live without a heart. You just can't."

She waves away his worries. "Oh, you needn't worry about the details. A little Bird tells me you were a butcher, so I know you have certain skills, and you don't have to take the whole thing, just half, like I've had done with the other, supposedly important, bits of me. I would so like to see my heart in a jar. It would be beautiful, wouldn't it? I could put it with my husband's. Did I mention that I kept his heart?"

"No. No you bloody well didn't."

"Oh, yes. I couldn't let that go. You've been in love – you know how it is. I couldn't find a way to keep it beating, but at least my heart and his would be properly together again. Please, do this one thing for me, to make up for all the nastiness of the past."

He pulls his hand free, stands up and shakes his head. "I can't. I won't kill you."

Minerva sighs. "But I won't die. Don't you see? It's only part of the heart. I'd have the usual nurses I hire to care for me. You wouldn't have to worry about me being in pain. I'd pay you enough to get your own surgery, get thin again, win your wife back. We'd both be with our true loves and, of course, you could have your cinema seat."

Minerva is surprised at how quickly Francis moves for a big man. The door slams shut behind him. She imagines him running, for the first time in a long time, all the way home, just like the littlest piggy. Old nerves wiggle a missing finger.

She sighs, reaches up and pats Bird's beak. "I had high hopes for that one. High hopes indeed. I suppose that's the last we'll see of him. At least our trips to the cinema will be more pleasant." She pats her chest. "I'll get you out of there somehow, heart. It will be so lovely to see you."

The next day, the cinema is showing *Brief Encounter*. "Your favourite, Bird, and Francis's. Shame he'll miss it," Minerva says, sinking into the seat and opening the seed packet. She tunes out the other pensioners and thinks how much better life was when everything was in black and white.

The seat behind her creaks. A meaty hand rests on her shoulder. "You're in my seat, old witch. I've booked my liposuction and a personal trainer. See you at your place later. Got my own knife."

A trickle of bird shit dribbles into Minerva's good eye.

~

Karen Jones' Biography

Karen Jones is a prose writer from Glasgow with a preference for flash and short fiction. She is addicted to writing competitions and is a perennial short-lister, though she has reached the prize-winning stage a few times, including with Mslexia, Flash 500, Words With Jam and Ad Hoc Fiction.

Her work is published in numerous ezines, magazines and anthologies. Her story 'Small Mercies' was nominated for Best of the Net, the Pushcart Prize and is included in *Best Small Fictions 2019*. Her stories have featured in the last two *To Hull And Back Anthologies*.

HAIL MARY

Highly commended story, by EJ Robinson

"Bless me, Father, for I have sinned."

"What is your sin, my child?"

The woman on the other side of the confessional grate is silent. This often happens, sins sticking in throats like fishbones. People make it inside the confessional box, then struggle to get the words out. I wait for the woman to speak.

When she does, the words burst from her like secrets from a child. *"I forgot to put out the empty milk bottles for the milkman last week, Father, so help me, God."*

I wait. Just in case that wasn't her confession. When evident it was, I say, "Well now, I'm not sure that not putting out the milk bottles qualifies as—"

"I did it deliberately, Father. My hubby asked me to do it, and sure didn't I not? After he'd asked me? That's a sin, Father, surely it is. What's my penance?"

"Penance would not be required in this instance."

When you've been a priest for the best part of a decade, when you know your brethren well, you recognise voices in the confessional. The woman's name is Mary Scanlan, and it shames me to admit, but I'm getting impatient with Mary. She's taken to making confession religiously the last few weeks since she's turned 50, each time presenting me with a soul as white as my cassock. Mary, bless her heart, is no sinner, and this apprehension displeases her something awful.

"I'm 50 years old, Father," Mary cries.

"Yes, my child," I say.

"How is it possible a woman of 50 has nothing to confess? Mustn't I have done something awful sometime? But I wrack my brains, and, *nothing*. I've done *nothing*, Father."

"This is no bad thing to—"

"I haven't lived, have I, Father?"

"Of course you have. You've been a good woman. Kind. Righteous. This is more than living, it is the *way* to live."

I hear sobs, muffled by palmfuls of tissues. I sigh,

feeling for Mary. Virtue, too, can be burdensome.

Then Mary, she says, "The milk bottles weren't the only thing this week, Father."

"No?"

"I've been... I've been having thoughts, Father."

"What kind of thoughts, my child?"

She sniffs. "Lustful thoughts, Father."

"Having such thoughts, my child, is not a sin."

"It's *not*?" Mary does not sound relieved. She sounds, in fact, like she's just stuck out her bottom lip and folded her arms.

"No. The thoughts are not the sin. Everybody has such thoughts, they're only natural. It's what we do with those thoughts, how we act on them, that matters in the eyes of our Lord. Do you understand?"

Silence. This is normal for Mary. But a minute ticks by, then two. It's so silent I can hear the tick of the watch on Mary's wrist. Then I hear her get to her feet and my compartment darkens as her figure blocks the light shining through the grate that divides my side of the box from hers. The door on her side opens, slams. I hear heels on flagstones and then, nothing. She's done a runner. Left St Patrick's in tears for want of sins on her soul. Again. I sigh. You want to help your flock in all their spiritual crises. There is plenty you can do for the bad, there is little you can do for the g—

The air in my compartment churns as a breeze floods in, the door slams, the lock twists and then a finger is on my lips and Mary's voice is in my ear whispering, "Sssh, Father. Ssssssssssh."

Have you ever been inside a confessional box? They aren't built for two. Well, they are, but they're not made for two bodies to fit inside one compartment. In the tiny slice of rectangle, Mary is pressed right up against me. It's the closest I've ever been to a woman and I'm frozen.

Rabbit in the headlights frozen.

And the only reason I realise she's unzipped me and yanked my trousers to my knees is I feel goosebumps coming to life on my thighs, but this only lasts the briefest of moments because Mary hitches up her skirt – *Sweet Jesus, she's come to church with no drawers on her* – and takes me in one fist and...

Holy Mary, Mother of God.

Her insides are brimstone hot, like she has a centre of sun and she has me by the backside with both hands and the confessional must surely to God be walking across the vestry from the force of her hips. This has never happened to me before. I see nebulae; I see the universe. I see God.

Then my guts burst in warming waves of effervescence, or so it feels, and Mary is off me and, wiggling her skirt back down, she nips out of the box back into the church, leaving me cassock asunder, quivering, exultant. I make out the sound of Mary's heels on the flagstones above the jackhammer of my heart in my ears, the unmentionable part of me still pointing up to God as though I needed a reminder He was watching.

Then I hear the creak of the confessional box door opening on the other side of the grate, the sounds of someone taking a seat and closing the door behind them, and I yank my trousers up and shrink back against the wall... But it's Mary's face that appears at the grating, and she's all smiles. Then she sits back out of sight and clears her throat.

"Bless me, Father," says Mary. "For I have, finally, sinned."

"Mary," I say. "Would you care to sin again next week?"

~

EJ Robinson's Biography

I'm a freelance tour guide and life-long writer. In 2010 and 2011, I had stories shortlisted in the 17-25 age category of the Wicked Young Writers' Award chaired by Michael Morpurgo, and completed Faber Academy's novel writing course in 2014.

On most days, I'm to be found in the taverns and halls and parks of London, telling the city's history to people from all over the world, always with a corner of my heart wishing I was at home writing.

SHORTLISTED STORIES

BOOK REVIEWS

Shortlisted story, by Brandon Robshaw

The postman stood on the doorstep with a large, yellow, bulging Jiffy-bag. Another batch of books to review for *The Independent on Sunday*.

"Thanks," said Bernard. As he took the parcel, he noticed that the postman had only half a beard. One side of his face was covered in dense black hair and the other half had only a few straggly wisps on a field of doughy pink flesh.

"What happened?" Bernard asked, sympathetically.

"What do you mean?"

"Well, your beard's only on one side of your face. Did it get burned off in a fire or...?"

The postman was staring with incredulous hurt in his eyes. "Most people are too polite to mention that," he said. "But you can't stop going on about it, can you?"

"Sorry, I didn't mean to..." Bernard said. "I was just—"

"Enjoy your *books*," the postman said. He turned and stalked through the gate.

Bernard went back indoors, annoyed with his own tactlessness, but also annoyed with the postman for making such a big deal of it. Yet, come to think of it, this wasn't the first time he'd asked the postman about his beard. He'd known the man for years and knew the whole story. His beard had been half-scorched away in a house fire which had also killed his black-and-white cat.

For some reason Bernard had forgotten, and not for the first time. In fact, he asked the postman about his beard every day. It was a compulsive pattern of behaviour. No wonder the guy was pissed off. *I must remember not to mention it next time,* he told himself. Just like he'd told himself all the other times...

Bernard put the Jiffy-bag on the kitchen table and opened it. Fragments of grey padding came out of the envelope and scattered, drifting over the table top like tumbleweed. He pulled the first book out, *The Necessity of Ritual*, by Conrad Bozo, and scanned the list of contents. 'The Prevalence of Ritual in Human Societies. Courtship Rituals. Rites of Passage. Food Rituals. Ritual in the Animal Kingdom. Can Plants Have Rituals?'

Oh, how fucking ridiculous, Bernard thought. *Plants having rituals, indeed.*

He opened the book at random and read, '...for it should be admitted straight away that the weaving of a spider's web satisfies many of our key criteria for ritual. It occurs in well-defined, unvarying stages. It is repeated. It serves a purpose connected with an essential act of spiders' lives, the getting of food. It is to be found, with certain variations, across many separate species, just as some human rituals are found, with local variations, across different societies.'

Bernard put the book down. He suspected some subtle pisstake. The book looked like a serious, scholarly study, but what if it was a hoax, designed to show Bernard up? On the other hand, he'd look like an ignorant philistine if he ridiculed it when it was a serious work. Well, he'd have to come back to that one.

He picked up the next book. It was oddly bulky, like a children's comic packed with free gifts. *The Story of Entomology*, by Dr Frederick J.F. Garvling, PhD, Emeritus Professor of Entomology at the University of Alberta.

Bernard scanned the blurb. 'A dazzling historical overview of entomological theories and discoveries, going back to the Ancient Greeks, giving full credit to the ground-breaking Arabic entomologists of the early Middle Ages who first distinguished between spiders and daddy longlegs and ruled that only the latter were insects, recounting the wonderful efflorescence of entomological studies during the Renaissance, and taking us right up to the present day and the progress in genetics made possible by the fruit-fly drosophila...'

Bernard leafed through and saw that at the end of each chapter there were live samples of the mini-beasts under discussion: little wriggling beetles and ants and flies in clear plastic sachets attached to the pages. You had to be careful not to close the book too vigorously or they'd all be crushed. It was a miracle that they'd come through the postal system unharmed.

As he watched, they began to struggle free, working their legs through gaps in the cellophane, tearing at it with their miniature mandibles. They were buzzing angrily.

A particularly large and horrible hornet burst free and danced around in front of Bernard's nose. The thing was enormous, like a yellow-and-black striped hummingbird. *If that stung you,* Bernard thought, *it would hurt insanely, like having molten metal injected under your skin.*

He retreated from the hornet, but it followed him, buzzing triumphantly. It was driving him from the room. He snatched the door open, darted through and slammed it behind him. He heard the hornet thud against the door, and then bang against it repeatedly, buzzing savagely.

Bernard was trembling and drenched in sweat. *Well, I'm not reviewing that,* he thought. *It's a stupid gimmick, including live insects in the book. Not just stupid, but dangerous. It's a fucking liability.*

Yet he had to get to work. The deadline was this afternoon and his editor, the crabby and demanding Alison Twite, had told him that if another review of his was late, she'd stop using him. He looked at the book in his hand, which he must have snatched from the table before his retreat. *The River,* by Dr Milt Spunkalot.

He flipped it open and read, 'A mighty river flows through the world every day, every hour, every minute, every second, a huge, thick, viscous white river with billions of tiny tributaries, every one of which spawns countless more tributaries, so that the river increases every second, every minute, every hour, every day. A massive torrent of semen pulsing forth from billions of cocks, spurting into hands, handkerchiefs, condoms, mouths, vaginas, anuses, splashing on carpets or bathroom tiles, a river teeming with life which never ceases or slackens, but only grows, pumping blindly, irresistibly, driven, urged, like a tidal wave, by a life-force, a will-to-be that knows no restraint or limits, instinctively searching to increase itself, able to waste trillions of its motile, questing denizens with dispassion, in the blind certainty that millions will find a target and continue to increase the total number of cocks from which more tributaries will flow...'

Hmm, Bernard thought. *Interesting, but a bit repetitive.* He'd say that in his review. Give it three stars. He couldn't quite see how Dr Spunkalot was going to get 400 pages out of this. An essay stretched out into a book. Could it be another hoax?

He heard an angry buzzing, which got louder very fast... and then that crazy hornet came zooming in through the window.

It looked even grosser than before – a flying pot of poison, too heavy for its own good, like a bomber-plane carrying a huge load that reduces its mobility and makes even getting airborne a matter of touch-and-go. It was *swaying* as it flew towards Bernard, as if the venom was sloshing about inside it, affecting its balance. It was purposely, single-mindedly out to get him, as though he'd perpetrated some deadly insult or injury that it must avenge.

Bernard swiped at it with the Milt Spunkalot book, but missed. It veered towards his face. For an instant he saw its hostile black eyes staring into his – deadly, pitiless, filled with unreasoning hate – and he had a momentary flash of how his own eyes must appear to it:

weak, watery, blue, straining with fear and anguish.

He gave a strangled yell and ran for the door. It didn't occur to him to stay and fight — to try to kill, crush, smear the hornet into oblivion. At least, it did occur to him, but only as an option that couldn't be entertained. The thing was too big, too stuffed with scalding poison. The idea of squashing it was too loathsome to contemplate.

His legs weren't operating with their usual fluency. His feet could not gain traction, as if the ground slipped away before he could really push against it. With infinite labour, he reached the hallway. The hornet kept pace easily, buzzing close to his ear but making no attempt to sting; it was teasing, taunting, tormenting him.

Bernard pushed open a door and found himself in a room he'd forgotten was there. There was a large, old brick hearth set into the wall, with a dark chimney, up which a set of rusty iron steps disappeared. Bernard remembered that this house had belonged to a Catholic family after the Reformation, and the steps led to a priest's hideaway. He'd be safe up there. The hornet would not follow. *They don't like dark spaces,* Bernard thought, *they like sunshine and flowers and open countryside.* Perhaps it was the creature's frustration at being confined that had so enraged it.

Bernard had to bend his neck and body awkwardly to begin the ascent. For a horrible moment he thought he was stuck — wedged in the chimney, breathing in soot, at the hornet's mercy. It could attack any part of him and he couldn't take evasive action. It could take its pick, sting his ear, the back of his neck, his hands, or it could fly inside his shirt and sting his nipples, or go up his trouser-leg and sting his genitals. He felt his testicles shrink up inside him, like toads burrowing into mud.

With a violent effort, he straightened up. His hands found the upper rungs, his feet the lower. He began to climb into the darkness. The hornet buzzed beneath, but didn't follow. It sounded angry, confused, balked of its target. *Hah,* Bernard thought. *That's outsmarted you. Stripy little bastard, flying pot of poison, like one of the winged evils that escaped from Pandora's Box.*

Bernard climbed faster. He had a deadline to meet. He had to get out of here and write those reviews.

*

The climb went on and on. Somehow, he must have missed the priest's hole, for he burst out of the chimney to find himself up on the roof, perched astride the narrow ridge, like Humpty Dumpty on his wall.

The wall was so high that the people in the street below were reduced to slowly-scurrying ants, and the cars crawled along the road like little shiny beetles.

Bernard crouched nervously, one leg dangling down each side, gripping the ridge with both hands. It was of rough, friable brick which crumbled under his fingers. A lazy shower of brick dust tumbled earthwards. Bernard forced himself not to look down. He had to concentrate on those reviews – he had only a few minutes before the deadline.

Luckily, he had his laptop with him. He balanced it carefully on the ridge, leaning on it with one hand while tapping the keys with the other. It was a dreadfully precarious position – at any moment he or the laptop or both could slide down and... He pushed that from his mind. Just get the review done and then, and only then, could he think about getting down from here.

He awarded Milt Spunkalot's book four stars. 'An

intriguing book,' he wrote, 'based on meticulous research. Dr Spunkalot possesses the mind of a scientist and the imagination of a poet.' *That was pretty well put,* Bernard thought. In his enthusiasm, he began to type faster, using both hands. Without a hand to steady himself he started to lean to one side. He leaned the other way, over-correcting, and almost toppled. He grabbed the wall with both hands – and jogged the laptop so it tipped and slithered down the steeply-pitched roof. It bounced off the guttering and came to rest on a window-ledge about three metres below.

Bernard groaned. Better if the thing had fallen all the way down and smashed into 10,000 pieces. Now he had to make a decision. Should he climb down and retrieve it? The thought made his bowels turn to water. But then, what could he do? He had to meet that deadline...

He groped in his inside pocket and found a notepad and a fat, silver fountainpen. The tried and trusted method of written communication, as used by Shakespeare and Milton and Dickens. Old school. Yes, why not? He still had no idea how he could deliver the reviews, but getting them down on paper was a start.

He began to write. The pen felt cold and chubby in his hand, almost wilfully inert. It was smooth and slippery and his fingers kept sliding down towards the nib.

'Dr Frederick Garveling's new book takes an unusual form,' he wrote. 'It's full of deadly insects and one of them attacked me and chased me up a fucking chimney...'

No, he couldn't write that. Too personal, not professional enough. Yet why shouldn't he make public his own experiences? Was he supposed to be some sort of unfeeling robot? Didn't people have a right to know about the dangers of this book?

The dilemma paralysed him. *All right,* he thought, *I'll leave that one for now.* He started afresh. 'Conrad Bozo's new book offers a challenging, post-structuralist interpretation of ritual...'

The pen deposited blotches of ink on the page, then ran dry and started tearing up little tufts of paper. *Oh, Christ on the crapper,* thought Bernard. *Doesn't anything work?*

A mood of exhilarated despair swept over him. There was no way he could finish this by the deadline, stuck up on the roof with a pen that didn't work properly. He was allowed to give up, virtually *required* to give up in a situation like this, wasn't he? What if he just stopped struggling, forgot his obligations – just relaxed, let go and fell into empty space?

His stomach tightened. No, he couldn't face that wild tingling in the gut, nor the exponentially accelerating approach of the ground, and he couldn't believe it wouldn't hurt, the moment of impact, when the back of his head hit the ground a split-second after his face.

He had to go on. 'Bozo's interpretation of ritual is...' Is what? Ingenious? Original? Stupid? Bollocks? A hoax, or a serious contribution to understanding? What, what, *what?*

The pen came apart in his hand. The section containing the ink-tube fell, skittering down the wall to the street below. Bernard looked at the bit left in his hand. It had a silver clip so that it could be attached to one's pocket, but what the hell was the point of that when the thing had no guts inside it? His fingers were drenched in ink. From far away he heard a church bell tolling.

That was it, then. He'd missed his deadline. The bell

sounded shrill and staccato, drilling into his ears vindictively.

Glancing down, Bernard saw that what he'd taken for insect-sized people on the ground were in fact insects, and an army of them were climbing purposefully up the wall towards him. Perhaps it was an optical illusion, but they all appeared to be licking their lips.

~

Brandon Robshaw's Biography

I'm primarily a children's writer. My book of spooky children's poems, *These Are a Few of My Scariest Things*, was published in 2017, and my Young Adult fantasy novel, *The Infinite Powers of Adam Gowers*, was published in 2018.

My day-job is being a lecturer for the Open University, in Children's Literature, Creative Writing, and Philosophy. 'Book Reviews' is one of a suite of stories I have written based on anxiety dreams, called *Bernard's Anxious Nights.* Some of these stories have been published – two in the anthologies *Fugue* and *Fugue 2*, and one on the MIR Online website.

DRIVING TO CHARTRES

Shortlisted story, by Christine Griffin

Malcolm was sorting through the romantic fiction section when he heard the library door bang. Gary, the delivery man from headquarters, pushed his trolley up to the front desk.

"Another fine crop for you here, Malc." He shifted his chewing gum from his left cheek to his right. "I ask you. Who reads all this stuff?" He plucked a large book from his trolley. *"Chartres Cathedral and the Wonders of the Medieval Mind."*

Malcolm tweaked his glasses and took the book from

him. "I believe it's a very nice place. I'd like to go there sometime."

"Where is it then?"

"France."

"Ah well you see the missus don't like foreign. It'll be Blackpool for us next summer again. Anyway, you'd have to speak the lingo. Kind of spoils your holiday that."

"Well maybe one day I'll get there. Who knows?"

Gary unloaded the rest of the delivery onto the desk. "Must drive you barmy, working in here. Anyway, can't stop." He winked. "See you next week, mate."

Malcolm watched Gary's van make its way up the narrow street to the main road. *It really is a lovely book,* he thought, as he flicked through it. A bit heavy going in parts but the illustrations were beautiful.

He wondered how you would get to Chartres. Plane perhaps, or train to Paris then change. The all-too-familiar taunting little voice struck up in his head. *Or here's an idea, Malcolm. You could drive. You could go to Folkestone, drive through the Tunnel and then – let's see – oh yes, you could drive to Chartres.* Malcolm tried to shrug the voice away, but it refused to go. *39 years old and still can't drive. I ask you.*

He sighed and switched on the computer to see that the book had been reserved by a Ms Olivia Wentworth. Not anyone he knew, but an interesting name. He wondered if she was some sort of academic at the nearby university – a lecturer maybe. He pictured her in a dusty lecture theatre expounding on the wonders of the medieval mind, while her pupils hung spellbound on her every word.

*

The telephone rang for a while before the answerphone kicked in. "Hi, I'm not here at the moment, but please leave a message and I'll get back to you. Promise. Ciao."

Malcolm was temporarily wrong-footed. His usual patter deserted him. "Oh, yes... er... library here. We've got your book on Chartres Cathedral. The one about the wonders of the medieval mind. You ordered it. So... er... see you soon."

You ordered it. Well of course she ordered it otherwise why would you be ringing? Honestly. Malcolm sighed as he started to tidy the children's section. School would be finishing soon and he'd need eyes in the back of his head when that lot arrived. There'd be no time then to worry about Ms Olivia Wentworth.

*

The next day, Malcolm was just about to start his lunch when he saw Mr Parkinson's bright yellow driving school car pull up outside, its large red L perched mockingly on the roof. Malcolm liked to think that he could get on with anyone, but he drew the line at Mr Parkinson. He cringed as he remembered the trial driving lesson he'd had a few years ago when he'd been told in no uncertain terms that he would never be a motorist.

A woman got out of the driving seat and ran towards the library. He was expecting to see Mr Parkinson's bulky figure in the passenger seat, but it looked as though there was no one else in the car.

"Morning. How can I help you? Is there a problem?"

She smiled and placed a huge striped holdall on the counter. "No, why should there be a problem?"

"Well, I just thought... what with there being no

instructor with you…"

"Oh, a lot of people make that mistake. No, I've come for my book. You left me a message. Olivia Wentworth."

Malcolm, you're gawping.

"Of course. Sorry it's just that…"

Just what exactly, Malcolm. What did you expect? Wrinkled stockings? Grey hair in a bun with a pencil stuck through it? A bag full of badly-written essays to mark?

"Let me get the book for you. I've had a quick look through it myself. It's beautiful."

"Well, it's a beautiful place. I can't wait to visit."

"Me too. I plan to visit myself." Why on earth had he said that?

"Anyway, I can't stop to chat. I've got a pupil in 10 minutes and it's her test tomorrow. See you soon. Ciao." And, swinging the bag over her shoulder, she went out, got in the bright yellow car and whizzed away up the road.

*

Somehow, Malcolm didn't feel like his lunch after that. He had the niggling feeling that he had got off on the wrong foot with Ms Wentworth. What did she mean about making a mistake? And that bit about the pupil and the test. That didn't sound the sort of thing a lecturer would say. He bit into his corned beef sandwich and decided that after lunch he'd give the foreign languages section a going over. No harm in keeping up his French – just in case.

*

He'd barely finished his lunch when the door swung open and Mrs Jenkins came in, shaking rain from her RainMate all over the magazine stand.

"Nasty out there, Malcolm. I need something romantic to cheer me up."

"Mrs Jenkins, can I ask you something? Only you know everything that goes on round here."

She looked at him oddly. "I take an interest in my neighbours, if that's what you mean. I hope you're not implying I'm a gossip."

"Oh no, really, no... it's just..."

Shut up, Malcolm. Shut up now.

She plonked her shopping bag down. "Cos I'm not. I'm known for my discretion. Anyway, what was it you wanted to know?"

"I wanted to ask you about Mr Parkinson."

"Him? Good riddance to bad rubbish is what I say. You know, he had the cheek to tell me once that I'd never make a motorist."

"Surely not. I find that hard to believe. But what do you mean 'good riddance'?"

"Well, he's sold up, hasn't he? Gone to live in Bognor or somewhere. He's sold the business to a nice young woman. Can't remember her name, but it's something to do with cooking oil."

Olivia Wentworth. Oh lord. Oh lordie, lord. She only owns the business. She teaches people to drive. And when she isn't doing that she goes to exciting places like Chartres. Probably drives herself there.

"Are you alright, Malcolm?"

"Why don't I help you to choose a book, Mrs Jenkins?" *And when she's gone, Malcolm, you need to put things right with Ms Olivia Wentworth.*

*

The telephone rang for a while before the answerphone kicked in. "Hi, I'm not here at the moment, but please leave a message and I'll get back to you. Promise. Ciao."

"Oh, er, yes. Good afternoon, Ms Wentworth. Malcolm from the library here. I feel I owe you an apology after our conversation this morning. You see, I jumped to a conclusion that just because you're a woman you couldn't be a driving instructor as well. Sorry. People jump to conclusions about me too and I know how annoying that can be. And I was expecting someone different, with a bun perhaps or something..."

There was a click. "Thank you and goodbye."

What? Now she'd think he was even more of an idiot. And you know what, Malcolm? There's no way you can wipe that message off. Why on earth had he mentioned the bun? Now she'd never agree to teach him to drive, which was what he'd been working up to when the wretched answerphone cut him off.

*

A week later, Malcolm was sorting a new delivery from headquarters when the yellow car drew up outside. As Ms Olivia Wentworth pushed open the library door, he couldn't help noticing that she was wearing her hair in a bun. She was also smiling.

"Good morning, Malcolm."

"Ah, Ms Wentworth. Can I help you with anything?"

"Well, yes you can, Malcolm, as it happens. I was giving Mrs Jenkins her driving lesson and we were talking about you. She tells me that you know French."

"Mrs Jenkins is learning to drive?"

"Yes."

"But Mr Parkinson told her…"

"I know."

"He told me the same thing."

"I know that too." She paused. "Malcolm, I have a proposition for you. I'll give you a trial driving lesson if you will help me translate this article I found in the Chartres Cathedral book. I think it's about the rose window." She handed him a creased piece of newspaper. "Shall we say tonight after the library closes for your lesson?"

*

Six months later, Malcolm stood in front of the great rose window at Chartres and marvelled – not just at the magnificent colour and architecture, but at the fact that he was here at all. His driving lessons had got off to a dreadful start.

"I don't often admit defeat, Malcolm," Ms Wentworth had said. "But I think Mr Parkinson may have been right."

His attempts at three-point turns and reversing round corners had been the source of much amusement in the town.

"Give it up, Malc, before you kill someone," Gary said, staring in disbelief at *Learn to Love Statistics – a Guide for Beginners.*

"You know, some people just aren't cut out for it," said Mrs Jenkins, grinding the gears as she drove away with a bagful of romantic novels.

The inner voice had plenty to say too. *As if someone like you could ever be any good at anything. I feel sorry for that poor woman.*

*

Yet four months after that, the dour driving examiner had handed him his pass certificate and he and Ms Wentworth had celebrated with a drink in the pub. And that's when the great idea was hatched.

She wanted to go to Chartres but couldn't speak French. He wanted to go to Chartres but was too much of a novice to drive. They would go together – as friends of course. They agreed that he might even drive some of the way to Folkestone and, in return, he would teach her some simple French phrases.

"Bit of a posh bird for you, Malc," Gary said when he brought in the delivery. He handed over *Elementary Algebra* as if it was about to burn his fingers.

"Warms my heart that does, Malcolm," said Mrs Jenkins. "It's just like that book you recommended. You know, the one about the posh lady and the wimpy man. Lovely it was. They get married in the end."

*

And as for the inner voice? The one that never had a good word to say? Well, that said absolutely nothing at all.

~

Christine Griffin's Biography

Christine is a Gloucestershire-based writer of prose and poetry. She has won several competitions both locally and nationally and in 2016 published a book of short stories. Her work has been featured on several occasions at the Cheltenham Literature Festival and on local radio.

In April '18 and April '19, she performed a selection of her work at the Cheltenham Poetry Festival. She was Commended in the 2018 Torbay Poetry Competition and, in October 2018, won the Gloucestershire Prize in the Buzzwords Poetry Competition.

FAT FRIEND

Shortlisted story, by Julie Bull

Being followed is an unnerving experience, particularly when your shadow is hell bent on encouraging you to make poor food choices.

"Have the lasagne," she says from behind, while you queue in the work canteen. "You deserve it."

She comes with me everywhere, even follows me on holiday, where I tend to hear this sort of thing.

"Food is a celebration, Joanna, one of life's pleasures. Enjoy it."

*

Flashback two years and you will find me in a very strange Skype conversation with a group of fat women and another person, Helen, who used to be fat but has gone so far to the other side that she is now working as a counsellor for a market leader in the slimming industry. She is listening to me very intently as I tell her about the crumpet I ate last night; about the way the butter sank into the dimples of the dough, allowing me to add some more butter.

"Can you tell us what was going through your head at that moment, Joanna?"

"Absolutely nothing was going through my head except how delicious the crumpet was."

Some of the other pixelated fat people titter a bit.

Helen the counsellor does not join in. I have displeased her. I could hardly tell her that Fat Susan made me do it though.

*

There are plenty of online meeting places for fat people these days; slim-mins, fat girl slim, weight-to-go. In these chat rooms you will find a rather large number of unhappy women congratulating each other because they chose to do the hoovering and drink a cup of vegetable stock instead of reaching for that chocolate bar which had been on their mind to the point of obsession for most of the day.

"Well done, hun. You are doing so well," say all the fat folk, people with usernames like goddess54 or icanandiwill.

These poor women. Of course, I am one of them. I am a fat woman. There is so much everyday, enduring shame in this fact that I cannot meet my own eye when

I look in the mirror; greedy pig, pie eater, fat slag.

*

It's nearly 70 quid a month to take part in Lyter-U. It's a fair chunk from my salary, but I am desperate, and cheaper alternatives, including those advocated by thin people – the just-eat-less brigade, as I have come to know and not love them – have failed. Lyter-U is the latest and the most effective very low calorie diet, well-reviewed in all the newspapers and with a multitude of celebrity endorsements, including a soap star who now wears a chiffon top and very tight jeans at all times.

The diet claims that it will 'completely re-programme my relationship with food'. In the How It Works section of the website, I read some of the science behind the stories. This information can be summed up as follows: you stop eating and instead ingest only powder and water; the powder contains everything you need in order not to die. You must also drink about a swimming pool full of water each day, which is to stop your bowels seizing up. Your body goes into starvation mode. After a short period, all appetite will vanish, freeing you to shrink.

I am very excited because the results are rapid and remarkable by all accounts. Not only that, the key to the sustainable results achieved by Lyter-U, is the counselling on offer. This unique psychological support helps you to understand why you are over-eating and how you've got to where you are. That is 16 stone in my case. My weight is a burden I want to put down. Helen is the counsellor that will carry me over into enlightenment – en*light*enment – get it?

*

Fat Susan laughs at my excitement. She knows the statistics, she says. "You will lose weight alright, and then you'll regain it – AND SOME."

She enjoys the emphasis she places on the last bit of this sentence and then she shakes her head, smiling at me as if to ask what it might take for me to face the facts.

I tell her to fuck right off and she replies, huffily, that there is no point in being slim if you have no manners.

*

The first weeks are hard. The powders bear no relationship to anything natural or edible, even though they are, somewhat cruelly, named after food: Thai Surprise, Chicken Supreme, Tex Mex Taste Bomb. I am by turns light-headed and beset by a hallucinatory headache that prevents me from functioning. I cannot sleep and I have no energy. On day five, my breath begins to taste of acetone and that is when I know that my internal fat burning furnace has been switched on. Bingo. I feel electric, and I begin to melt.

After that, I am troubled only by halitosis and constipation – very small prices to pay for the weight that begins to fall off me, leaving my trousers comically large. I enjoy the privation, the suffering. As far as I am concerned, it is nothing less than I deserve. I lurk on the fora, comparing starvation and temptation levels with my Lyter-U sisters, hoping I might find someone else who has a fat friend but I find no one.

There are bad times in these early months. There are moments when the memory of food punches through my starvation like a fist through a paper screen. Then there is the crumpet lapse. I watch other people sitting at tables, chewing, tasting, raising a fork to their lips with an insouciance that I marvel at. After three months, my sleep is punctuated by dreams of liver and onions, fingers of shortbread, baked potatoes the size of a babies' heads, split wide open and covered in melted cheese.

*

Helen is keen to link my eating issues with an absent parent or other 'emotional trigger'. She looks sceptical when I tell her that my parents, Lyn and Roger, are alive and well and living in Hemel Hempstead and that we like each other and always have. Even I begin to think that I must find something in my family history, or my early childhood experience that will unlock the mystery of my love of bagels and my hatred of all forms of physical activity.

One day, I happen to mention that I was pretty slim until I hit adolescence and her eyes light up. She suggests that the fat I accumulated was a way of insulating myself against becoming an adult. I buy this, mainly out of relief that I have satisfied Helen's quest, but also because it makes me seem complex rather than merely greedy. I dare not admit to Fat Susan in case I am sectioned.

*

As I begin to lose more weight, people who haven't seen me in a while – and there are quite a few of them – fail to recognise me. My face in particular has emerged from the rings of fat that previously circled my neck and chin, so that I look not much like the former me. I look more serious somehow and, I like to think, more intelligent. Fat Susan tells me I have aged, that my face is becoming just a tad haggard. She enquires after my performance at work because she says she has noticed that I am not as mentally sharp as I used to be.

"Or funny, actually. You used to be funny but you've lost your sense of humour."

"Good," I say. "It weighed a ton."

She offers me a chocolate mini roll.

"Go on," she says. "Treat yourself."

I stick two fingers up at her as she turns to put the kettle on and begins laying out the mini rolls on a decorative plate.

*

Men begin to look at me – total strangers in the street. My ability to turn heads is such a novelty that I court it, swinging my hips and smiling at passers-by. But while I enjoy being objectified by anonymous men, I feel no particular urge to follow through with any real life relationships.

I recognise this is a problem and so, at 10 stone, and at Helen's suggestion, I make it a project. I start dating at the same time as I begin to eat food in a way resembling a normal person again. There follows an untold number of assignations with men I have met online. During these encounters, I push food around on my plate like it is toxic waste and find I have nothing much to talk about. My fat past is the one thing I don't want them to know about me. "I used to be obese," is not, I figure, the best prelude to a night of unbridled passion, but I am sad to realise that I have no other stories to tell. In shedding more than half of my body weight, it is as though I have also cast off any sense of who I am. Fat Susan is right, in a way. I am not sharp or funny, just formerly fat and now empty.

I am still getting slimmer. Fat Susan dances behind me as I fill bin bags with clothes that don't fit me anymore. She gyrates her hips as she gives me a pep talk about the folly of thinking that changing your appearance can change how you feel inside.

"Look within," she says, panting from her exertions and pointing at her sternum.

It is a wonder that I have not hit Fat Susan before this particular evening, but when the moment finally comes, it is all the more satisfying for the build-up. I land a slap on her face so hard that it makes my hand sting. She looks shocked and hurt. She weeps a little bit before suggesting we make it up over a small glass of Baileys and a choc-ice.

"They go really, really well together," she says, blinking back tears.

*

The surgeon is very careful to explain the full body-lift procedure to me. He has a diagram in front of him onto which he draws lines with a dark marker pen showing where he will make the incisions. He can cut away all my loose skin, do a bit of liposuction while he is at it, and then it is only a matter of me being in agony and taking to my bed for a few weeks. The cost is an eye-watering £14,000. I thank him for the initial consultation and emerge into the waiting room to find Fat Susan waiting for me.

"Are you fucking kidding me?" she says, looking up from her copy of *Glamour* magazine.

"What?"

"You think you can get rid of me that way?"

*

I decide against the operation in the end. Some of my skin gets a bit tighter naturally because I have come to love running and I take up Pilates. The other thing that brings my skin back to some degree of tension, is that I put on some weight. These things together seem to balance out the worst excesses of my body's memories and distortions. What surprises me is that I am not unhappy to see my thighs regain some of their plumpness. My breasts become fuller, I go up a dress size. I am nothing like as fat as I was before, but as I see my curves return, I am not afraid. I decide I can live with them. Fat Susan is still with me but she is quieter.

One day, I catch sight of myself in a shop window as I walk down the High Street. I am wearing a navy wrap-around dress and wedge heels and my hair is longer than it has been for ages and I have allowed it to wave, as it has always preferred to do. I realise as I pass my reflection, that I like what I have seen. I am 32 years old, I am strong and healthy and, the other thing I never thought I could believe is that, I am sexy. There is no one else who can confirm this for me, but that doesn't matter because I know it to be true.

*

Four months after this revelation, I am in the south of France, sitting on a terrace, drinking Kir and eating olives, when it occurs to me that I haven't seen or heard from Fat Susan in a long while and somehow I know that she is not coming back. Her disappearance makes me feel a little melancholy from time to time in the week that follows, but the man I am spending my holiday with more than fills the gap she leaves behind.

When he is not reading the crime fiction to which he is addicted, he often makes me laugh 'til I cry and every afternoon he takes me to bed, or I him, because this is nothing if not mutual. The sex is not chaotic, nor is it orderly. Each time it is its own great surprise.

At the end of these sex siestas, we leave the hotel to eat, finding a new restaurant each night and delighting in the flavours of entrecote, fish stew, mousse-au-chocolat. We eat everything with a relish that makes our dinner an almost sacred ritual. In the mornings, we swim far out to sea as the day dances on the water and my body feels strong and alive as I float on my back and contemplate the breakfast which awaits me back at the hotel.

Apart from a brief relapse before my wedding, I never weigh myself or go on any kind of diet again and yet I maintain a healthy weight for the next two years. Food is something I enjoy cooking and eating. I like it to be fresh, wholesome and delicious but, beyond that, I do not give it much attention.

*

Then, a year into my marriage, it happens – my body begins to expand again. I stand in front of the mirror in my underwear as I get ready to go out for dinner on our first wedding anniversary and I can see that my stomach is bulging so that my pants roll over at the top. My breasts will not be contained in my bra but seem to be bursting out of it like round, blue-veined moons. My face too, looks plump.

I am growing. I am what my mother calls showing. I am once again in the throes of something that seems to be out of my control. Only this time, it is something I have no desire to reverse because, to coin a cliché, it is a miracle I am witnessing here.

I put my hands on my belly, and appraise the body in front of me with a cautious admiration. The baby is due in March.

~

Julie Bull's Biography

Julie Bull is a writer who lives in South London. She used to be a Whitehall civil servant but has now accidentally retired and is using her time to write short stories and reinvent herself as a freelance journalist. She is also currently writing a novel about growing up in Leeds in the 1970's.

She hates hiking and moths. Her work has appeared in MIR Online, Retreat West and FunnyPearlsUK.

FIVE TOES, AND SO ON

Shortlisted story, by Dan Purdue

All through the introductions, even when he was shaking the surgeon's hand, Steve couldn't drag his gaze from the foot. It captured his attention entirely, although not by being a particularly remarkable foot, not unusually big or small, nor hideously deformed. It wasn't doing anything inappropriate or unfootlike, either. It was just lying there, being a foot. *And maybe that's the problem,* Steve thought, frowning at the thing. *It's literally* only *a foot.*

The foot lay upon a sheet of blotting paper in a blue plastic tray on a metal table in the centre of the room. It stopped being a foot, stopped in fact being anything at all, six inches above the ankle. Someone had bandaged the end of it, forming a neat dome where the shin bones would have poked out. A small but troubling brownish stain had formed in the middle of the bandage.

With considerable effort, Steve looked away and pulled his notepad and pen from his bag. Ted Watkins, his colleague from Sales, was in full flow, reeling off some beer-sodden tale from his days playing semi-professional rugby. Steve's limited experience of orthopaedic surgeons suggested they could be separated into two factions – the gung-ho, action hero types who spent their free time jet-skiing or howling about on high-performance motorcycles, and the fearsomely intellectual ones, fluent in half a dozen languages and capable of completing *The Times* cryptic crossword before they'd even finished the day's first cup of coffee. Steve wasn't sure which he found more intimidating, but today's surgeon slotted neatly into the first classification, unleashing a deep, braying laugh at each depraved twist and turn of Ted's story, which now seemed to involve urinating from the top of a multi-storey carpark. The surgeon's assistant, a willowy lady with greying hair gathered into a loose ponytail, shook her head and went back to laying out a selection of surgical instruments along one edge of the table. And, with that, Steve's attention was drawn once more to the foot.

His boss had assured Steve that attending the laboratory session would be good experience. A 'valuable opportunity for learning and development', or some such corporate-speak intended to justify unshackling Steve from his desk for the day. He would need to be comfortable with such potentially grim and gory things if he fancied promotion to bioengineer in the future, after all. Most of the senior product designers had been less supportive, seizing the opportunity to tease him, recounting their own cadaveric encounters reeking of putrefying flesh and sights that even the strongest stomach struggled to cope with. Steve hoped they were exaggerating. At home, his girlfriend had done her best to equip him with what she called 'coping strategies' – although these mainly revolved around having a packet of extra-strong peppermints to hand, and not standing too near anything with sharp corners, in case he fainted.

That morning, as he drove to the hospital, Steve had tried to prepare himself for the weeks of humiliation that would accompany his return to the office if he ended up passing out or throwing up. But it turned out that a foot by itself was... weird. He didn't feel any horror or disgust, only a strange and powerful sort of fascination. Aside from whatever was seeping through the bandage there wasn't any blood. There wasn't even much of a smell. After all his trepidation, in some ways it had turned out to be a bit of an anti-climax.

The surgeon was helping the company develop a new plating system for metatarsal fractures. Steve had designed the screws that held the plates in place, his first major project since joining the company as a graduate engineer. His boss told him he'd done a good job, but when the prototype screws finally arrived from the workshop, Steve had felt disappointed. After all the time and effort that had gone into them, they just looked like screws. There wasn't really anything else you could say about them.

Ted brought his story to a suitably unsavoury

conclusion, and then the still-chuckling surgeon and his assistant pulled on latex gloves. To his relief, Steve wasn't offered any. He didn't like the idea of touching the foot with its baggy, greyish flesh. The salesman excused himself to make some calls, and the physicians set to work. Steve watched the dance of scalpels, saws, and drills as the surgeon created an injury the foot had never sustained, before making a repair that could never heal.

Afterwards, they all reconvened in a staff room to discuss the procedure over scolding hot but tasteless vending-machine coffee. The surgeon said the plates worked well but suggested some minor improvements to the design. Steve wrote them in his notebook. "How were the screws?" he asked.

The surgeon frowned. "The screws? The screws were fine." He shot a glance at Ted, who pulled a face and did a pantomime shrug. Steve looked away, a blush searing its way across his face.

The surgeon stood up, saying he'd better get back to the day's list. "After all," he added, "I do like some of my patients to have a pulse." His assistant rolled her eyes.

There were handshakes all around, and then Steve promised he'd be in touch and said goodbye. He found his way out of the hospital and sat in his car, uncertain where he was supposed to go. Taking the drive into account it would be too late to return to the office but too early to go home. He set off anyway, feeding his ticket into the machine at the barrier in a kind of daze.

He couldn't get the foot out of his mind. As he drove, he found himself wondering what kind of life it had led, back when it had been part of a person. Before it became only a foot. All the steps it had taken, how it might have ached after a long day. Had it been ticklish? Where had the other one ended up? It had been small, a woman's foot. Back in its prime, had she decorated its nails with brightly coloured varnish, worn a toe ring, an ankle bracelet, perhaps? When she had signed her body over to medical science, had she imagined one of her feet going on to play a potentially pivotal role in a young design engineer's career? He suddenly felt guilty that he couldn't clearly remember whether it had been a left or right foot, although he wasn't sure what difference that made.

The traffic thickened as Steve neared his home. He watched as the lights ahead cycled through red, red-and-amber, green, and back to red again without anybody moving an inch. Sighing, he switched off the engine and gazed along the row of shops on the opposite side of the street. And that's when he saw the foot again.

No – it wasn't the foot, it was a different one. This foot was huge, for a start, and healthy looking – sun-kissed and lovingly pedicured. It was on a poster advertising the new season's sandals, hanging in the window of a shoe shop. As the traffic began to move forward again, Steve slotted his car into a parking space at the side of the road and got out. He crossed the road, his eyes fixed on the poster, only dimly aware of the blaring horn of the driver who'd only just braked in time to avoid flattening him.

*

Inside the shop, Steve drifted around the shelves, trying – for reasons he couldn't quite define – to guess the type of shoe the foot might have worn. He stared at sandals, espadrilles, Doc Martens. Though he could picture the foot standing up in them, his imagination stubbornly stopped short at that bandaged stump. He wasn't sure if that was the problem, but none of the footwear seemed quite right. Steve picked up shoe after shoe, turning them in his hands, examining them from different angles, feeling their weight.

The longer he spent looking, the more intensely he felt a rising pressure to choose the right shoe. But how could he do that? He knew so little about the foot. And he wanted to do it justice, if he could. It didn't seem fair to condemn it to an imagined lifetime cooped up in a nondescript, own-brand trainer, or countless steps haunted by the echoing slap of a flip-flop. No, he wanted, needed even, to find something with a little flair to it. Something that would imbue the foot with a bit of, well, life.

He was clutching a bright red stiletto when a sales assistant asked if he needed any help.

"Just looking," he said.

The assistant offered him a hesitant smile. Steve looked again at the high heel in his grasp, tried to calculate how long he'd been loitering among the racks of women's shoes. He felt an alarming certainty that she suspected he was either a transvestite or some kind of fetishist.

He grinned at her, worried that made him look guilty, glanced away, coughed an unconvincing cough, and then tried again. He nodded towards the shoe. "I was only…" He rubbed the back of his neck. "Actually, it's a funny story."

She looked expectantly at him, but he couldn't think of a follow-up sentence that wouldn't at some point lead to him mentioning part of a dismembered corpse.

Which, surely, would be much worse than anything she might be imagining. He felt trapped, cornered. Steve gripped the shoe, his knuckles whitening, as a dizzying wave of panic surged up inside him.

*

Afterwards, on the drive home, Steve's mind gradually drifted away from the foot. The vivid mental reconstruction that had seemed permanently seared into his memory seemed to soften and disperse like smoke. Even when he deliberately tried to summon up an image of the thing, the details were hazy and indistinct. The foot he'd remembered so well a matter of hours ago was slipping away, becoming an amalgam of all the other feet he'd ever seen. He felt a curious sense of loss.

Steve pulled up outside his flat and switched off the ignition. He sat for a moment, taking long breaths and staring out through the windscreen at nothing in particular. His brain pulled itself, almost reluctantly, up and out of its increasingly foggy recollections of the foot.

A moment later, he turned, looked at the box sitting on the passenger seat, and began to wonder exactly how he would explain to his girlfriend the gift of an expensive pair of red stilettoes he knew full well would neither suit nor fit her.

~

Dan Purdue's Biography

Dan Purdue lives and writes in Leamington Spa. His occasionally published, sporadically prize-winning fiction has appeared in print and online in the UK, Ireland, Canada, and the United States. His stories have found their way into *The Fiction Desk*, the *2016 To Hull And Back Short Story Anthology*, *The New Writer*, *Jersey Devil Press*, *The View From Here*, *Every Day Fiction*, *Southword*, and *The Guardian*.

His work has won prizes in a variety of competitions, including The HE Bates Short Story Award, The Seán Ó Faoláin Short Story Competition, The James White Award and Flash 500. His work has also featured in an English study guide, and been performed live at the Berko Speakeasy. One of his stories has been broadcast on hospital radio, although the fact that this has never happened since suggests the medicinal benefits of his fiction are, at best, negligible.

HAPPY AND GLORIOUS, LONG TO REIGN OVER US

Shortlisted story, by Adrian Hallchurch

The Home Secretary asked if our meeting could be held in private.

"Highly irregular," I said.

She arched her plucked eyebrows plaintively. I'd heard a rumour that something rather sensitive was about to land on my desk and I asked Angus, my principal private secretary, to leave the room.

"But Prime Minister, the Civil Service code says..." he stammered, but stopped short of laying out all the niceties of protocol that it was his professional and legal duty to uphold. Like a well-trained poodle, he usually did what was asked of him.

"Thank you, Angus."

He scuttled through the open door, closing it behind him, and the worry lines that ran across the Home Secretary's forehead softened.

"Would you like tea, Home Secretary?" I asked.

"No, thank you, Prime Minister, I think we need to get to business."

I glanced out of the window. April snows. Thick tennis balls of snow. This was one of the coldest and longest winters I'd ever known – certainly the worst since 2069 – and we could really have done without the news that I half-knew the Home Secretary was about to deliver.

"It's true then?"

"I'm afraid it is, Prime Minister."

"Who confirmed it?"

"It's all being done through the King's lawyer, Stephen Doddsville – a weasel of a man."

"It was a private discussion, I take it? No notes or recordings?"

"Absolutely. We met at his rather grand townhouse in Shoreditch."

"Well then, you better tell me what those royals are up to."

"They've had enough. As simple as that. They want

to be an ordinary family. An end to the pomp and ceremony. An end to being the clowns in the circus. Those were Doddsville's words, not mine..."

As the Home Secretary spoke, I found my eyes drifting towards the window, mesmerised by the hypnotic fall of the snowflakes, and felt grateful that I didn't have to leave Number 10 all day.

"No more pretending to be interested in half-naked dancers in some long-forgotten corner of the Commonwealth. No more being imprisoned by photographers and security guards – Doddsville's words, again, Prime Minister. He just kept repeating that they wanted to be an ordinary family."

"Poppycock. As long as the world keeps turning, they'll never be an ordinary family."

"Quite true, but they think that if they end the thing now then, maybe not their children, but their grandchildren, might be able to live more normally."

"With bills and mortgages, and having to do some proper work for a change. Well, I'm guessing that if King Ralph wants to abdicate, that's his prerogative. Let him. Didn't Edward VIII abdicate? Over that American woman... Simpson."

"Yes, but..."

"We just go to his son."

"Prince Sebastian won't do it."

"You don't know that."

"I'm afraid I do, Prime Minister."

"Then we'll crown his daughter, Princess... Princess..."

"Princess Sophia won't do it, either."

"But she's only five."

The Home Secretary looked at her feet. She was wearing new suede boots that would suffer in the snow as it turned to slush. I felt like advising her on that point.

"They're all in on it. Cousins, second cousins, aunts, uncles. They've signed a document of abdication. A long list of earls, dukes, duchesses... reads like *Burke's Peerage*."

"Burke's what?"

"Never mind. I saw it in Doddsville's house – 57 signatures in green ink."

"I'd like to see it. Did you make a copy?"

"No, that awful lawyer wouldn't let it out of his hands." Her voice was losing the tone of calm authority that I usually associated with the Home Secretary.

"Are you sure you won't have tea?"

"Actually, Jasmine tea would be nice. No sugar."

I buzzed Angus and asked him to arrange our drinks.

As we waited, I found myself staring at the oil painting of Margaret Thatcher that hung above my desk. She looked resplendent in a chalk blue suit, golden hair perfectly coiffured and her whole being radiating a fortitude that was beyond words. She would never have stood for this.

The drinks arrived.

"When's all this going to happen?" I asked.

"Our lawyers are looking at it."

"We'll be wiped off the map at the election."

"I'm afraid so, Prime Minister. And it probably hasn't helped that you chose that royal crest for our new logo."

"No, quite... a huge misjudgement on my part."

She noticed me staring outside again.

"Horse Guards Parade looks lovely," she said.

"Lovely," I replied.

Then she explained that a parliamentary Bill to abolish the monarchy would be supported by the opposition. "They are republicans, after all," she added.

"What about Royal Assent?" I laughed at my own joke, though the Home Secretary only frowned.

"Though we may need a referendum," she said, "and people might actually understand what they're voting for this time."

"Not like that old Brexit business. No wonder there's never been one since."

"It didn't turn out that badly... except for losing Scotland. That was a bit careless."

"It wasn't really a loss, though, was it, Home Secretary?"

She laughed this time. Poor old Scotland was begging the World Bank for yet another emergency loan.

We agreed that we needed a report from the lawyers before we could consider this properly and I suggested we adjourn.

I called Angus back and he took notes while we discussed the terrorist bomb that had caused Nelson's Column to collapse on a dozen Korean tourists the previous week, and then the Home Secretary left.

I'd been pondering the issue all day and, as darkness was falling, I put on my cosy fur hat that had been a present from the president of Eastern Russia and went for a lone stroll around the lake in St James's Park. I'd spent a lifetime scheming my way into Number 10, and I wasn't about to give that up now, royals or no royals.

I shouldn't have been too surprised, of course. The last time I'd seen King George, on his deathbed, he'd confided that he'd never trusted his oldest son.

"The fool's more interested in his bloody family," he'd whispered.

At his funeral, I'd felt an icy breeze gust through

Westminster Abbey as the coffin had arrived. I wondered whether this was some kind of grisly warning from the spirit world that I should have heeded, even though I'd never believed in such things.

The next day, the Home Secretary arrived wearing a crimson dress she knew I rather liked. Angus brought me coffee, and Jasmine tea for her, and then dashed out.

As she sat down, I noticed white smudges on her black boots where the snow had left its mark.

"Bad news I'm afraid, Prime Minister."

"I know. You should never wear suede in the snow. It gets ruined."

Her cheeks turned the colour of her dress.

"I've had a report back from the lawyers. All hush hush, of course."

"Of course."

"They say that if King Ralph abdicates, we have to consult the lineage until someone agrees to be monarch. We're not allowed to pass a law."

"So who are we left with?"

"It will be a 'Queen Constance'," she said slowly.

"I like the name," I replied, optimistically.

"Though you won't like that she lives in an eco-community on the edge of the Spanish Sahara – in a tent."

I shuddered and spilt coffee on my pale grey trousers.

"Damn."

"Are you OK, Prime Minister?" The Home Secretary pulled a tissue from her bag, knelt in front of me and started dabbing my thigh with slightly too much enthusiasm. At the same time, my eyes locked on Margaret Thatcher's passionate blue-grey eyes, and feelings that were not at all helpful to the situation began to take hold.

"I'm OK, I'm OK," I said, lightly brushing the Home Secretary away and hoping she couldn't smell the sweat seeping from my armpits.

As I stared at the stain, I asked whether this tent-dweller had any intention of agreeing to become our Queen.

"Well, she refused to sign the declaration. Weasel thinks she quite likes the idea of living in a palace."

I slumped in my chair.

"It gets worse. She's an anarchist – Mi5 has a file on her already," the Home Secretary continued.

I inspected my trousers to make sure nothing too obvious was happening down there before standing up to allow air to circulate around the damp patch.

"The public won't stand for anarchists in Buckingham Palace. We can have our referendum and be done with it."

The Home Secretary smiled sarcastically.

"The election will take place next year, Prime Minister. If King Ralph abdicates, along with his 56 closest heirs, we'll be destroyed."

I told the Home Secretary I needed more time to think.

"Very well, Prime Minister, but there are rumours on social media. My office is working round the clock to knock them down, but we don't have forever."

I didn't sleep well that night and had a vivid dream that was, without doubt, the result of the endless coverage of the Trafalgar Square bomb. I woke up covered in sweat. My wife said I'd been shouting. But my terror had been so real that it sparked an idea that could possibly save our party.

Even before I'd drunk my first coffee of the day, I summoned the Home Secretary.

When she arrived, I noticed she was wearing shiny black boots made from patent leather. Although they seemed new, and she was walking awkwardly, I thought her very sensible, and nearly said so.

I'd told Angus he could arrive late, so we didn't have to worry about that minuting business.

"I'll get straight to the point, Home Secretary. If the royal family decides, as it seems to be doing, to become an ordinary family, it won't be entitled to many things that it enjoys by nature of its privilege. For example, it won't receive the same levels of personal protection. The taxpayer will be saved the fortunes spent on armed bodyguards and the fastidious arrangements we make to ensure their safety, wherever they go – the sniffer dogs, the litter bin checks, the snipers on rooftops, the reams of intelligence pored over by Mi5."

"Yes, Prime Minister, that's right. Of course the King and his immediate family can expect the same level of protection for their lifetime, and…"

I coughed, and she fell silent.

"The snipers on rooftops," I repeated tersely, looking out of the window. "It's unfortunate, and, I suppose, a regrettable by-product of their status that members of the royal family are always in the cross-hairs of some terrorist organisation or other. Always. It's a great shame, don't you think?"

"I see, Prime Minister."

I turned to see her looking down at her new boots, her nose reflected against the toe as a monstrous mound of flesh. I stifled a laugh that would have needed explaining amidst the enormity of what I'd just asked of her.

"I think our discussion is at an end. A business delegation from Indonesia is visiting in 10 minutes to discuss how it intends to run our ambulance service."

"Good day, Prime Minister."

She walked slowly to the door and went through it without looking back.

"Good day, Home Secretary."

Events moved faster than I could have possibly imagined after that. Two weeks to the day, I joined the Home Secretary for a press conference outside Number 10.

The snow had gone but the temperature was still close to zero and most of the journalists and camera crews were wearing hats and gloves. As I walked to the microphone, I could see the smoky clouds of their breath rise into the air. I doubted many had slept. They would have been working through the night. This was the biggest story for decades. A story that would have ramifications for decades to come.

I cleared by throat and located my deepest, most serious voice.

"Ladies and gentlemen, it is with a sombre heart that I am addressing you today. The utter shock and deep sadness I feel, I know, is the utter shock and deep sadness that we feel as a nation.

"This time, the terrorists have struck at the very foundation of our country, to our very idea of order and civilisation. They have struck at the beating heart of the traditions that have bound us together for centuries. This barbaric attack by people who have no respect for human life or for the freedoms we cherish. This is an atrocity beyond belief. Not since Earl Lord Mountbatten was murdered, almost a century ago, have terrorists been successful in an attack on the royal family.

"You already know the grim facts, but I will repeat them now, so that there is no doubt. At around 7.30 yesterday evening, there was a bomb blast outside the royal residence at Windsor Castle that claimed the lives of King Ralph, Queen Dominique and their daughter, Princess Sofia. Prince Sebastian survived and I am pleased to be able to tell you that doctors say he is out of danger, though he may lose a foot."

My lips were drying up in the cold, and I licked them while I surveyed the rows of faces of men and women. Their mouths didn't smile but their eyes let me know that I was giving them what they needed for their headlines and deadlines.

I thought about that last word, and beat down the urge to smile.

"We must remember that despite all that it means for our country, at the heart of this tragedy is a family. An ordinary family, like my family and your family. Though the difference is that through an accident of history this family finds itself a target for terrorists. Remember that a son has lost his mother and father, a brother has lost his sister..."

This was Churchillian. Thatcheresque, even. The election wasn't until next year, but it was already in the bag. Another five years as Prime Minister. Oh yes.

"And like all families struck by tragedy, they need time to grieve. Members of the media, I ask this of you, that during the coming weeks you curb your professional instincts and let the story come second. I beg that you allow them privacy."

I paused. They would do nothing of the sort, of course, but people would remember my humble pleading.

"This is all I have to say this morning. The Home

Secretary will recount the incredible work of the emergency services and explain the progress the police and security services are making to bring those responsible to justice. Our nation is suffering, but this will make us stronger. Terrorism will never defeat us."

There was some clapping from the journalists, which made a pleasant change.

As the Home Secretary stepped onto the podium, I gave her a gentle squeeze on the elbow. Her stern gaze held firm, but, deep inside, I knew she was glowing as warmly as I was.

~

Adrian Hallchurch's Biography

I used to work as a journalist and I've done a lot of writing in my time – for newspapers, magazines and websites, and have even had a few (almost a handful) short stories published in anthologies.

Writing is my hobby, and I've been lucky enough to have been part of the Original Writers Group for the past 10 years, meeting many other aspiring writers of all ages, shapes, sizes and abilities, working on a seriously wide variety of projects. We meet in the children's nursery at the Battersea Arts Centre in south London, surrounded by giant bees and ladybirds, something like going through Alice's looking glass.

I produced a couple of seriously poor novels a few years ago and, thankfully, I never found an agent and they weren't published. These days, with the demands of a full-time job and a six-year-old daughter, I am writing mainly short stories. More recently, I've found myself writing more satirical pieces, including this one about politicians and the royal family. It's not a laugh-a-line comic romp, but if the dark, gentle humour entices a smile or two among readers, my work is done.

MISTER SWITZERLAND

Shortlisted story, by Susan Bennett

Wash Separately

If he were a shirt, he would have to be washed separately. His label would declare him a delicate garment to be protected from other shirts, unable to withstand the rough and tumble of the washing machine. He would require hand washing in tepid water, flat, shaded drying and a cool iron, though it wouldn't get the wrinkles out.

Do Not Soak

On wet days, he won't set foot outside the house. He has less water resistance than a cheap watch.

The first sign of winter sees you decorating the stairs, twisting picks of plastic holly and little golden boxes with glittering red cherries around the balustrades because he takes exception to the grey light and demands that you should cheer him. You plant plastic flowers in the garden because he finds the view from his window too depressing to be borne.

The wearing of dark clothes provokes accusations that you are ruining his mood. "Bright colours suit you," he says.

Mild Detergent Only, Do Not Bleach

Bright colours suit you, but not on your face. Your lipstick is *too* pink or *too* red. Your hair is *too* dark or *too* light. Everything about you is either *too* or *not quite*.

Your hair is not your hair but *the* hair, as in, "There's something about the hair that isn't quite right."

He is a beige gourmand. Food must never be *too* either. The slightest slip with the oregano provokes days of recriminating glares and accusations of strong flavours. He measures jam for his toast with a teaspoon. Each slice may have exactly one spoonful. No more. No less.

A single square of chocolate or solitary lolly satisfies him.

"One is enough," he says. "One is plenty."

Spin Gently

If you are sad, he scowls and says you worry too much. "I want you to be happy."

But not too happy. When you laugh aloud, reading about the widow fined for dancing on her husband's grave, singing 'Who's Sorry Now?', he accuses you of disturbing him and stalks into another room to read the newspaper in solitude.

Designed in Australia

You know he has come home because the house feels emptier.

His mother calls on the business line in his study so there's no chance of you picking up the phone. She hasn't spoken to you since the Christmas when you drank seven beers and made that crack about the mantelpiece portrait of him winning the baby contest, when he was awarded the title of Bluest Boy.

"Good job it wasn't a personality contest, Myrtle. He would have been disqualified."

Made in the U.S.A.

When your own mother criticises the state of your marriage, you point at the framed photograph on the wall and let her have it.

"It's your fault, Mum. You let a politician kiss me when I was a baby." Not only did your mother allow the politician's curse, she courted it. The photograph captures the aftermath of the headbutt: the other baby airborne and the contorted, pained expression of the rival mother as she falls to the ground.

The look on your infant face says it all.

Somewhere out there, you know the grown-up baby who escaped the politician's lips is having sex with George Clooney and eating chocolate biscuits for breakfast – nice ones, and one for each hand.

You have no doubt that you were cursed by that politician's kiss, though in your more candid moments of introspection you concede that the Kennedy family could legitimately say the same of you.

Lukewarm Rinse

He is deeply suspicious of the toilet, knows it conspires to betray him. He uses the full flush because, he says, he doesn't trust the half flush. If the mere prospect of faintly tinged water makes him swoon, you wonder how he manages to get the undiluted article out of himself without fainting; speculate, in your idler moments, that he may rig up a hoist using his handkerchief to allow him to pee with eyes closed.

Do Not Wring

At night, he tip-toes to the bedroom and retires without saying goodnight so you won't know he has gone to bed and try to join him. He says he doesn't touch you in bed because you are too cold. You lie awake remembering another man who kissed you goodnight and held you, who always made sure you were warm.

Sometimes, when you wake and see Mister Switzerland on the other side of the bed, it is all you can do to catch the words 'I'm sorry, I've forgotten your name' before they leave your mouth.

Do Not Tumble Dry

Back when he still did touch you, you had to enquire whether he had climaxed. There was no way of guessing. He gave no clue other than not moving anymore.

On his birthday, you give him a Far Side card, depicting the moods of an Irish Setter.

Lucky for you, he doesn't get it.

The problem with sorrows: the more you try to drown them, the harder the bastards swim. In the mornings, you ponder how much was too much last night, try to remember the time when less than too much was enough. You know that for every third glass of wine you drink, a fairy in the World Health Organisation keels over dead.

100% Polyester

You never could settle on a way to introduce him to other people, couldn't bring yourself to call him your boyfriend, husband or partner, because he was never any of those things.

There had been no first flush of mad excitement, no tortured dinners you couldn't eat for thinking about him. No phone calls where you both refused to hang up first or retrieved the handset from the cradle, holding your breath and straining to hear if he was still on the line – or even, just holding hands. You had sex without becoming lovers, without being laid to waste by insupportable desire or insatiable lust, or dreaming about the first time you would do lovely, lusty or daring things to each other, for each other, or together, when you would shock him on your knees or he would rock you on your back. No courtship, no kinship.

The Earth didn't stand still so much as burp.

He took you to lunch once. You invited him back to your place; learned during his first visit of his intention to return the next weekend and every weekend thereafter. One day, he suggested getting married without actually proposing; he had bought the ring months before and assumed you would be happy to 'come along for the ride'.

Somewhere along the line you started referring to him as 'the other half', not because he completes you, but because he takes up half of the bed that could otherwise be yours.

Wash with like Colours

One night, you wake with the impression that your side of the bed looks like the aftermath of a car crash. The bedclothes are a sculpture in shadow. In the rounds and folds of the covers you see the spatchcocked panels of a crumpled car: boot lid and tyre well, quarter panels with wheel cut-outs, concertinaed doors, crushed registration plates, an erupted steering column, the rear view mirror angled like a broken hat.

And you remember that other man.

While the other half sleeps soundly on his smooth side of the bed, you remember, with shame, that other man.

You recall him pulling the blankets up when you tossed them off, but had forgotten how carefully he went about it. The rustle of the sheet close to your ear brings it all back, the memory slicing you like a sweet scythe.

All through the night he patrolled for escaped limbs

and, on finding one, he crept the covers back over you, so gently, so quietly, trying not to wake you, never knowing that you woke to feel his tenderness, that you felt his smile in the dark when he thought he'd gotten away with it, and that you, spooned against him, were smiling too.

May Be Dry Cleaned

In his sleep, he looks vulnerable, almost boyish. Watching him, you surprise yourself by finding some residual well-spring of feeling for him. Yes, you decide, a small part of you still likes him, but only when he is asleep.

You slip from the bed quietly, as he has trained you to do through the years. The only time he ever looks at you with an assimilation of love, when he rewards you with a genuine smile, is when you are quiet. How he delights in your silence, congratulating you when you leave the house in the morning to do the shopping without disturbing him. "You were as quiet as a mouse, I didn't hear a thing," and he looks at you then like another man might look at a woman who presents him with a longed-for child, or a chest brimming with treasure.

On silent feet, you cross the bedroom to look at love in the mirror, see yourself throughout your marriage – your harlequin clothes and pale, nude lipstick; your smooth, dun-coloured hair; your neutral blusher and beige eyeshadow – and decide that bright colours might well suit you, but you would prefer black.

~

Susan Bennett's Biography

In her first job, Susan Bennett sold large knives, handcuffs and replica pistols to complete strangers. Many years later, it occurred to her that some of those nice people may not have been buying these items for joke gifts, as they claimed. Maybe they weren't even nice.

PLAY MISTY FOR ME

Shortlisted story, by Martin Strike

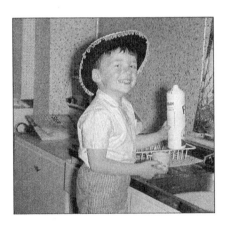

I sidle along the cheese aisle as slowly as I can. Some lunchtimes, they've put Miss T Cleavers at the end of cereals and other days by canned fruit and veg. But today it's dairy products, and I feign interest in a wheel of Camembert. I hold it up, pretending to read the sell-by date, while through my fingers I'm gazing at her graceful arms, all whitish and slender, as she scans people's groceries.

I always go to her till and buy the same things for

lunch – a pint of milk, a jacket potato and a steak – which I take back to the office staff room to microwave.

I'm trying to build up some muscle. Misty (my nickname for Miss T Cleavers, as is shown on her name badge) wouldn't fancy a 20-year-old weakling like me; all feet and nose. To be honest, a microwaved steak is as chewy as a plimsoll, but at least the water that broils out of it lubricates the potato a bit. I don't like milk either, but still drink a pint for its body-building properties – not that it's built anything yet.

I join Misty's queue. She's beautiful. She's got the half her hair that isn't black dyed white. It curls round her head perfectly, like a sleeping badger on top of a walnut whip. There's not a hair out of place, as if it's moulded through a giant Play-Doh barber set.

Denise at the office says, "Hair isn't meant to be perfect," as she watches me crush mine down with my brush, desperate for it to lie flat while it insists on hampering my love life by springing up at the ends. Denise's hair behaves itself and she gets asked out all the time. How come everyone else finds dates and hair so easy? I'm not that terrible a person, am I? I'd treat a girl like a princess. OK, so I hate clubbing and Ed Sheeran, but I think I'm OK really, just boring, I guess. Denise is always on at me to try a dating app, but it's just not for me – I'm too scared. She says she'll be my 'mating mentor', but the thought appals me.

I'm getting nearer the front of Misty's queue now. She picks up a loaf. How I'd love her to grip me like she does that seedy bloomer. I hear the customer accuse her of squeezing his bread. She can squeeze my bread any time, turn it to crumbs even, like she turns me to crumbs. I'd love to step in and defend her honour, but I can never get my words out when I'm near her.

Anyway, she doesn't know who I am, of course, and he's bigger than me.

The man loads his bag and goes. It's my turn. As my steak, milk and potato trundle along the conveyor, I feel the lump build in my throat.

"Did you hear that bastard?" she says.

"Err, yeah," I stammer back, trying to sound indifferent and cool. I can't believe Misty's spoken to *me*.

"How can I pick up bread without squeezing it? I've got hands, not flippin' flippers."

"Ha, yeah," I add, not really understanding her point and thinking that, hands or flippers, I think they're gorgeous.

"Put this on the end of the belt." She passes me a closed sign, like it's a token of our love. Has she waited to serve me before she goes for her break?

Of course, I'm happy to oblige and enjoy the rest of my transaction more than ever, in silence apart from her, "That's £8.97," and with me captivated by the octopus tattoo on her wrist and her black lipstick, luscious as a Pontefract cake.

Having insisted that she put my 3p change in the charity pot to show I am kind and generous, I stand back to allow her to exit her booth. Then it strikes me. She has legs. I've been yearning for her for so long but it hasn't even crossed my mind what they look like, and now here they are. Both of them. They're shorter than they might have been, which does not seem to match the slenderness of her arms, but I don't mind. She has tiny, angel's feet, in cute DM's.

"You following me?" she says as she strides towards the door. I didn't even think she knew I was there, as I try to keep up and view her recently discovered legs.

"Erm," I splutter, feeling rather caught out.

"Thought so," she says. "You can do something for me."

"Yeah, no prob," I say. I would do *anything* for her.

"Get fags for me at the kiosk. I'll, err, pay you back later."

"Don't worry about that," I say, "I'll buy them for you. As a present."

"OK then. Marlborough Lights. I'll wait here."

She stands over by the trolleys while I queue. I can't help my voice trembling as I ask for the horrible things, and can't believe how expensive they are when the lady says, "That's £8.35."

Misty smiles at the cigarettes as I bring them over. I see her teeth for the first time and realise that despite weeks of coming in my lunch hours hoping to see her, I have never seen her smile. They are perfect, petite teeth, each separated by a small gap, giving the appearance of a well-tended war cemetery.

"You can smoke them with me if you like. Round the back."

"OK then." I've never even had a puff, and feel like a sailor being lured by a Siren's call to a rocky and potentially cancerous end, but there is no way I am going to pass up this opportunity.

I push through a break in the chain linked fencing after her, down a worn, rubbish strewn path to a clearing in some wasteland. We sit on the bare earth, surrounded by a thousand cigarette ends and some evidence of previous illicit camp fires. She breaks into the packet's plastic wrapper with her keyboard teeth, and I watch her elegant fingers reach in and raise a cigarette to her lips. It bounces up and down in her mouth as she asks, "Got a light then?"

"Oh, don't think I have," I say, padding my jacket pockets for a lighter I know not to be there. I'm fearful that this will mark the end of our date before it's even begun, yet partly relieved that I can't be cajoled into smoking.

"Thought not," she says, and pulls one from her pocket.

"Great."

Having lit up and drawn a couple of deep puffs, as if replacing all unwanted oxygen with nicotine, she holds out the packet to me.

"Not for me, thanks," I cough, as her fumes reach me.

"Yeah, I'm trying to give them up too. It's a 'mare isn't it?"

"Tell me about it."

"How many were you on?"

"Sorry?"

"Fags, you idiot. Before you stopped. I'm on 20, but it used to be more like 30."

"Yeah, me too. 'Mare." *30.* That's nearly 15 quid a day. Even my steak lunch isn't that much. I hope my horror doesn't show on my face.

She leans back. "My old mum would kill me if she found out."

"Yeah. Mine too." I'm really struggling to think of anything to say that would not condemn me as being the non-smoking wimp I am.

"We got something in common then."

"We have?"

"Of course. We both hate our mums." How sad, I think, that anyone should hate their mother. Mine's annoying, sure, but... Misty looks up at me. "What's your name then?"

"Just John. Boring, I'm afraid." I immediately wish I had lied and called myself something cooler, like Caspian.

"Better than mine, Just John. Bet you can't guess what it is."

"Erm, Tracy?"

"Cheers, you tosser. You think I look like a Tracy?" I'm mortified that I've upset her, but she continues. "Don't laugh, but its Titania. My dad's a right cock and likes Shakespeare. *Midnight's Daydream*, or something. That's why I have it on my badge as 'Miss T' – it saves all the piss-taking."

"It's a beautiful name." I can sense myself blushing. Could this be the opening for me to overcome my shyness and tell her how amazing she is?

"Nah, it's shit," she says.

"If I were you, I'd call yourself something like, oh, I don't know – say, Misty?"

"Now you're taking the piss." She lights another cigarette.

I'm horrified. "No, no. Misty. Miss-T. Get it?"

"Ha. That's a bleedin' cat's name, you knob."

I'm a bit disappointed by this. I had imagined calling her 'Misty' on our wedding day.

"You're weird," she says. "You buy me fags then take the piss out of me name. Then squirm like a fish trying to get out of it."

I struggle to find something to say other than querying whether fish actually squirm.

She looks at me and says, "You can kiss me if you like, Just John."

"OK," I say, trying to keep calm while my internal organs start gyrating so much they could win a disco-dancing competition. It suddenly feels very hot.

"Don't sound too keen about it, will you?" she huffs, but before I can answer, she leans forward and clamps her lips on my face.

I always thought kissed lips would feel soft, but hers are hard and muscular, like a calamari ring. Her mouth tastes of burning ash and I'm not sure I like it even before her tongue comes into my mouth like a dragon rising from the catacombs of hell.

I lean back as her lips push harder and yelp as my hand presses on something clammy.

"What the fuck?" she says, and gets up. I look back and see my hand pushing into the cold, raw lunchtime steak in my bag.

"I'm sorry," I say, "but I've got to get back to work or I'll be in trouble."

"Fine, suits me," says Titiana. "Weirdo."

I can only agree with her assessment of me. I run back from lunch after an extemporary snog with the girl I thought could be mine, shaking. Denise could sense that something was up. I tried to explain why it had seemed so awful, but I didn't understand it myself.

"What's wrong with me, Denise?"

"Nothing," she says. "You stay being you. You'll find a girl whose kisses taste of M&M's in time, don't worry."

*

I've not had a microwaved steak for about six months now, nor been anywhere near that supermarket. Denise was right, although I'd say her kisses taste more of Jelly Tots.

~

Martin Strike's Biography

Martin approves of all wastes of time in life, except golf of course, and opts to fritter away his own valuable hours adding bunkum to his blog, The Newbury Short Story Teller, while mulling that his pen cannot be mightier than the sword, as he would rather be poked in the buttock with a biro than a rapier any day. To avoid any uncomfortable misunderstandings, Martin used a laptop to write his Amazonally available book, *Preposterous Tales from the Newbury Short Story Teller.*

Should you approach Martin, don't mention that he once had a dog that didn't have a nose. How did it smell? Well, it couldn't; it didn't have a nose. When not writing or daydreaming, Martin lives with wife, Joanne, and Mrs Pastry, a fully-nosed cat, near Newbury library where he can roam free from his life-long fear of milk-based puddings. Oh yes, when not mentioning the dog thing to Martin, don't be carrying a blancmange.

Long-listed for this very competition in 2016, and even adjudged runner-up in 2017, Martin is very appreciative of the hard work from Christopher Fielden and his drones in providing us this opportunity to inadvisably share the foul workings of our minds.

www.thenewburyshortstoryteller.wordpress.com

QUEEN OF THE MERMAIDS

Shortlisted story, by Steven John

When anyone who cared to listen asked about her working life, Daphne would say it had been both rewarding, and professional. When they asked in what field she'd practised, she said she'd been a hotelier. At this point her listeners, who had perhaps pictured her in a barrister's wig or a doctors white coat, now re-imagined her at the helm of a five star hotel in London's Belgravia. They envisaged her as the charming hostess, in demure and seamless control of all the hotel's moving parts, faultlessly attentive to her customer's desires.

In fact, Daphne had owned, and single-handedly managed, a six bedroomed, one star hotel, a five minute walk inland from the Grand Pier at Weston-Super-Mare. A town synonymous with the dirty weekend, the donkey derby and the ditch brown waters of the Bristol Channel.

Many visitors to Weston-Super-Mare would have said that Daphne's accommodation was more 'Bed and Breakfast' than hotel, but Daphne bridled at the epithet.

"Bed and Breakfasts do not put cotton napkins in silver napkin rings, nor do they put Earl Grey teabags in the bedrooms," she'd say.

She did have a point. If eyebrows were raised at her description of hotelier as a profession, Daphne would explain that running a hotel required many of the same skills as one of the so-called professions.

"It demands the discretion of a priest, the firmness of a headmistress and an accountant's eye for the bottom line," she said.

After 25 years as hostess at her 'La Bella Vista' hotel, Daphne had tried to sell but had reached the conclusion that the market for small, independent hotels in Weston-Super-Mare was at rock bottom. The best offer she'd received for La Bella Vista had come from the town council. The public sector was in the process of 'redeveloping' the over-supply of holiday accommodation into affordable housing for low-income families and hostels for the homeless. Weston-Super-Mare council had offered her half of what she paid for La Bella Vista back in 1975.

"If you call that 'town centre regeneration'," she'd told the man from the council, "I'm Queen of the

Mermaids."

Fortunately, Daphne had paid generous monthly amounts into a private pension for the past 25 years. She didn't need to sell La Bella Vista to afford her one-bedroomed apartment in the Cotswold retirement village complex, with its liveried mini-bus to the supermarket and aqua-aerobics in the complex's indoor pool. She put La Bella Vista into lavender scented, boarded up, mothballs.

Three years later, Daphne woke up in her retirement apartment and decided that she was bored. Bored with afternoon ballroom dancing classes, bored with TV quiz shows in the communal lounges and bored with her neighbours not waking up – ever.

Daphne parked her little car on the double yellows outside La Bella Vista, and retrieved her black-market blue badge from the glove compartment. The padlock on the front gate was rusty but the key worked. The few bare paving slabs either side of the short path to the front door were deep in litter and underneath a front window someone had spray-painted a woman's face performing fellatio on a giant penis, with the words 'A Stick Of Weston Rock'. Daphne stopped a moment and tutted, although there was nothing in that department that shocked her. Her tuts were more for her wall.

She opened the front door and pushed aside a drift of envelopes and flyers. Her 'Vacancies'/'No Vacancies' sign still hung from the staircase newel. She re-hung it from the hook on the door and turned it to 'Vacancies'. She flicked on an electric light switch. Nothing. When she'd left the Cotswolds that morning, Daphne had arranged for a carpenter to come and remove the boarding but she'd forgotten about the electricity. She carried a torch for emergencies in her handbag.

Daphne went from room to room on the ground floor. A few pieces of furniture had been left; a telephone table in the hallway for the 'Resident's Only' telephone. Her list of 'Useful Numbers' was still taped to the wall; doctors, cinema, taxis, etc. Daphne didn't list restaurants, they were the competition. In her tiny office, her metal filing cabinet, with 25 years of correspondence, in alphabetical hanging files, was still there. The wheels of her office chair had worn holes in the lino.

Her decorative theme in the residents' lounge had been hats. There were framed pictures of hats on the walls, china hats on the sideboard and hats woven into the carpet. A large collection of hats, including a bishop's mitre, a tam-o'-shanter, a chef's toque, a Turkish fez, a cowboy's Stetson, all still hung on their hat pegs. She lifted her favourite hat off the wall over the fireplace; a circus ringmaster's top hat. Daphne put it on and cracked an imaginary whip.

"It's good to be back," she whispered.

Then, she went to the kitchen, lit two candles and put them on the worktop with the unopened post. She went to fill the kettle but there was no running water. She tried a ring on the stove but there was no gas. Daphne went to her office to call the utility companies but the phone was dead.

Ideally, she'd have checked into a neighbouring B&B but money had become a little tight of late. She could sell her Cotswold retirement apartment but that wouldn't happen overnight. Daphne decided to make do with the menus and toilets of local cafés until things were straightened out.

The largest bedroom in the house, room one, had been the honeymoon suite, with a glimpse of the Grand

Pier. Daphne had always placed an arrangement of flowers on the windowsill for genuine honeymooners. She hadn't troubled the florists very often.

She went from room to room in numerical order – that's how she'd done the housekeeping, one to six, vacuuming, topping up the toilet rolls and making the beds.

In each room there were remnants. The built-in, mahogany veneer bedside units were all still there, Gideon bibles in the drawers, coat-hangers in the wardrobes with La Bella Vista embossed onto the plastic frames. Dead flies were thick on the carpets and the ceiling corners were grey with cobwebs. In room three there was a decomposing mouse in the en-suite. In room four there were a handful of pornographic magazines in a bedside cabinet. It wasn't an unusual find after a businessman had checked out. Daphne flicked through. Many things had changed in Daphne's 75 years, but sex wasn't one of them.

The Grand Pier lit the long strings of fairy lights above the evening strollers. The torch batteries were on their last legs and so was Daphne. In room six, she stretched out on the mattress, buttoned up her coat and tried to remember the last time she'd lain there.

Gilbert Aitken. He had always asked for room six. Gilbert had been a travelling salesman for a dehydrated vegetables business. He was on the road five days a week, different hotel every night. He'd step into The Bella Vista in his pin-striped suit and glimmering black shoes. He signed the register with a silver fountain pen and always wrote a glowing report in the visitor's book.

Perhaps it was on his third or fourth visit that it happened. He'd been her only guest that night.

"Would you care to join me for a nightcap in the

residents' lounge?" he asked.

They both chose a glass of port. Gilbert had told Daphne about his wife and four children and the food factories he visited with his samples of dehydrated vegetables, from Cornish pasty makers in Truro to haggis makers in Inverness. Daphne told Gilbert about her childhood in her parents' pub in Bristol. About how she was left on her own in a little flat above the pub from the age of six with nothing but a doll for company.

Before Daphne and Gilbert knew it, they were half way down the port and it was past midnight.

"I'm so sorry for keeping you up," he said, squeezed her knee, rose unsteadily from the sofa and asked if Daphne could possibly have a quick look at the radiator in his room.

"It's running rather hot," he said.

That was the first time Daphne had had sex since she'd lost her virginity to the vice-captain of the darts team on her parents' bed above the pub.

What Gilbert didn't know was that the only sexual knowledge Daphne possessed, beyond the missionary position, was what she'd seen in the pornographic magazines left behind in the bedrooms.

"I may have to visit the West Country more often," Gilbert said later that morning, when she served him his full English.

Whilst he ate, Daphne went to her office and prepared his bill. In the row marked 'Extras', Daphne wrote 'Laundry and Ironing £30.00'.

*

Daphne woke with a start from her half-asleep memories. She was shaking with cold. 10-o-clock. She'd slept for longer than planned.

The local shops would all be closed. With her dim torch, she went into room five and lifted a rug off the floor. That would have to be her blanket. She went back downstairs, lit another candle on a saucer and carried it to the residents' lounge. In the little mildewed fridge behind the corner bar, she found a bottle of Indian tonic water and a packet of salted peanuts, both years past their best before dates.

Gilbert had been the first client of her other, new found, profession and he partook of 'Laundry and Ironing' on every subsequent visit. Daphne's problem had been how to communicate her new service to other guests. After trial and error with plenty of cleavage and short skirts, she'd found a subtle physical approach worked best.

When her male guests sat down for dinner and she spread a cotton napkin on their laps, she would give their crotch a gentle squeeze and say, "If there's anything you'd like served in your room, just leave the napkin on the chair and I'll be up later."

Soon, Daphne was practising her secondary profession on a nightly basis and, although she still thought of herself primarily as a hotelier, her 'extras' were showing better return on investment.

Daphne looked again at her collection of hats on the wall of the resident's lounge. The traffic warden's cap, the horse-riding helmet, the bullfighter's sombrero and the circus ringmaster's top hat (with whip) had all been good for business. Her prices had gone up according to the amount of theatre required.

Daphne took the candle back upstairs to room six. She spread the rug over herself and closed her eyes. The market for a 75 year old whore was going to be niche. Daphne wondered whether she could 'madam' one or two younger girls on a room rental basis to bring back the customers. She could offer apprenticeships.

She thought back to the heydays of her business. There were nights when she'd entertained groups of men in the residents' lounge; some music, a themed striptease, cracking the circus whip over her group of tamed, naked 'lions'. Her rather explicit floorshow, 'Queen of the Mermaids', with audience participation, and prize for the biggest trident, had stretched company credit cards to their limits.

Daphne closed her eyes and drifted off. Downstairs in the kitchen, a lit candle toppled into the pile of unopened post. A flame caught hold of an envelope corner. The envelope caught hold of other envelopes and flyers advertising pizza deliveries and political parties. The flames swept up a wooden wall unit until they were licking at the door of room six.

As Daphne began to snore, she could feel the heat of the men's bodies in her hotel beds, she could smell the smoke from their cigars, she could even hear the laughter and crackle of expectation.

~

Steven John's Biography

Steven John's writing has appeared in *Burningword, Bending Genres, Spelk, Fictive Dream, EllipsisZine, Ghost Parachute* and *Best Microfiction 2019*. He's won Bath Ad Hoc Fiction a joint record six times and has been nominated for BIFFY 2019.

He lives in The Cotswolds, England. Steven is Fiction & Special Features Editor at *New Flash Fiction Review*.

Website: www.stevenjohnwriter.com
Twitter: @StevenJohnWrite

SAX APPEAL

Shortlisted story, by Renée Boyer

When they offered me the job, I'd been out of work six months. 'Failed composer turns back to music teaching' is a tired trope, one I resisted as long as I could. But I was down to my last can of beans and starting to look sideways at the cat's tuna and gravy. I mean, it's just fish, right? I wouldn't have turned them down if they'd told me I had to shove a bugle up my arse and play reveille every morning before school assembly.

So, first day in the staffroom this woman wafts up to

me, all scarves and beads and smelling like she's just emerged from a spice drawer. "You're the new music teacher, yes? I'm Juliana," she cries, swooping on me like a nesting magpie, and planting kisses on both my cheeks. "It's so nice to have you on board."

I have no idea who she is or what she wants, but it doesn't take a genius to figure out she isn't the algebra teacher. Art, I guess. Or drama.

"I'm the drama teacher," she trills. I doubt the woman ever does anything so mundane as simply speak. "We'll be working together on the school musical."

This is unwelcome news. "I don't think so," I reply. "I'm just here to teach. I don't do musical theatre. More of a classics man."

"You mean Gilbert and Sullivan? Rodgers and Hammerstein?"

"No. Schubert and Stravinsky. Rachmaninoff and Handel. Even wrote two symphonies myself. You won't have heard of them. No, musical theatre is a little... frivolous for my tastes."

She laughs, a peal of tinkling bells. Until that moment, I didn't think anyone had a laugh like tinkling bells outside of Harlequin paperbacks. Gives me an instant headache.

"Oh, you're funny Mr...?"

"Peter. Peter Dawson."

"Well, Mr Peter Peter Dawson, we're going to get to know each other very well. We've chosen the production already. *Chicago*. You know it." It isn't a question.

"That toddlin' town?"

She grimaces. "No. That song isn't in it. It's ridiculous. Every time I say *Chicago* to anyone they break into a chorus of 'Chicago, Chicago (That Toddlin' Town)'. That's a Frank Sinatra song. Nothing to do with the show. No, *Chicago* is a musical set in a prison, following the story of two women who've been accused of murder and are facing the gallows. It's hilarious. Normally, we'd involve the musical director in the decision, but you wouldn't believe how long it can take to get the rights."

"Wait – musical director?" But she's gone, leaving nothing but sandalwood in her wake.

By the end of the day, I've petitioned the head of music, dean of arts and principal, to no avail. They aren't without sympathy but it's clear: I am the lamb to the slaughter. And less than three weeks later I find myself handing over care of my cat to the beheadphoned teenager next door and packing my bag for four days and three nights of Drama Camp.

If I'm wrong about the afterlife being nothing but dirt and worms, my personal hell will be this: eternity spent in a wilderness lodge 12 miles southwest of fuck knows where, with no one for company but 47 hysterical teenage actors, an apathetic band, and a drama teacher.

I'm assigned the room next door to the camp manager, a corpulent specimen whose wheezing suggests I'll be treated to a veritable symphony of snoring through the paper-thin walls.

Once room allocations are finalised, we assemble in the main hall. After a rousing speech, "Call me Juliana," separates us into our requisite cohorts: main cast, chorus, band. I gather my crew and take stock. Three pimply horn players, two flautists, a couple of clarinets, one each on violin and cello, and a surly pianist. I'd met them all during auditions, of course, but this is our first meeting as a collective. I'm not overly confident. Nor, it seems, are they.

I try to rally. "Right, troops. This is all new at the moment, but I am confident that with a lot of hard work and practice, you all have the ability to be... well, at least mediocre. We're going to be onstage for this show, so you need to get it right or we'll be in *treble*." No laughs. Motivational speaking isn't my forte. I give it a final shot. "So, let's show these warm props," I gesture towards the actors, "what actual talent looks like." Not even a crouching ovation. "Turn to the overture please."

They stir themselves with all the enthusiasm of a legless man at a shoe sale. We run through a lacklustre tune up and I'm about to launch into the overture when I pause, curtailed by a familiar musk. Juliana has materialised behind me, clutching the arm of a tall, dark-haired young man with an oleaginous smile and an instrument case tucked under his other arm. Clearly, a number of girls in the room find his self-consciously over-styled look attractive. The boys too – this is drama camp after all. The chorus pause their raucous game of 'Zip, Zap, Boing', and the room seems to hold its breath.

"Peter. This is Sebastian. Your saxophonist." Juliana's purple talons dig into Sebastian's arm, somewhat possessively.

"You must be mistaken, *Juliana*," I say, enunciating each syllable. "I don't have a saxophonist. As I recall, there wasn't a single sax player in the entire school."

"Yes but this is *Chicago*. It's a *jazz musical*. You can't have a *jazz musical* without a saxophone."

"Actually, you can. There was no saxophone in the original 1974 Broadway production." I don't know if this is true, but I'm betting Sandalwood doesn't either, and there's no internet out here in the backend of nowhere for her to check.

"Well, in the 2019 McKellar High production, there will be." Juliana's mouth is pinched tight as a cat's arse, and she shoves Sebastian forward with such force his smile nearly slides off his face. "I've called in a favour. Seb is a former pupil who has recently been signed by Artista Records for a solo saxophone album, and his YouTube channel subscribers include none other than Kenny G himself."

Her eyes spark and I bite back a snigger. Even Sebastian looks embarrassed to be associated with Mr Elevator Muzak G.

"We are very fortunate to have Sebastian with us, and I expect you to make him feel welcome."

I roll my eyes, but motion Carlene, first clarinet, to shift over a chair and make room. "Fine. There's one problem though," I smile, but only with my mouth. "We don't have a saxophone score."

"Don't be so goddamn difficult, Peter," she snaps, showing her temper for the first time. "He can share one of the clarinet scores."

She stalks off back to the gawping chorus before I have time to explain that that genuinely won't work – from the size of the case he's carrying, I assume Sebastian's an alto saxophonist. It's a completely different key.

Sebastian fixes me with his smile. I can feel my pores clogging. "No worries, man. I can transpose in my head." Of course he can. Seb the golden boy.

He shuffles his chair in closer to Carlene to share her stand. She flushes a fetching shade of fire engine, and brushes hair out of her eyes.

I lift my baton, but Sebastian holds up his hand, and

stands.

"I just want to say that I'm really honoured you're allowing me to play," he says, fixing each member of the band with his beaming teeth. "We may not get flowers on opening night, or have fans lining up at the stage door, but I want you to know that what you do matters. The jazz is in the music. You can *be* the jazz hands." His smile increases a few watts. "I believe in all of you."

I snort, deciding whether to cry or throw up, but then I see the band. They're all sitting straighter in their seats, rolling their shoulders and radiating a timid but definite energy. The oily little bastard's done it.

We launch into the overture. It's a disaster. Out of tune and out of time. But Sebastian, unfortunately, is brilliant.

However, over the next three days, the band, despite my misgivings, starts to improve. Carlene glows under Seb's tutelage and her breathy notes take on some substance. The horn players are in competition as to who can get Sebastian's coveted 'thumbs up' the most and actual notes begin to emerge from the formerly flatulent brass section. Sebastian even stays up late to practice with Violin and Cello, which means the camp caretaker stops popping into our practice room looking for the injured cat.

I don't hold out much hope for the flautists, who seem more interested in swapping gossip and hairstyling tips than playing music, but on day two, Seb stops practice and says, "You know, girls, when Kenny commented on my latest video, he said, 'What I love about Seb's playing is his *focus*.' He italicised it. For emphasis. *Focus*. I think you two have the potential to be great – but you have to work on that *focus*." Not only do they listen, but from then on, anytime anyone starts slacking off, one of the others will hiss, "Kenny G says *focus*." It'll probably be my epitaph.

By the last day of camp they may be no Duke Ellington's Orchestra, but they're a hell of a lot better than the cast. I feel strange. It's either a heart attack, or pride.

We do a mid-afternoon stumble through of the whole farce in preparation for show-and-tell for the school's senior leadership, who'll be coming to watch later on: a camp tradition, apparently. Midway through her seminal monologue, Roxy falls to the ground sobbing, "Jesus wouldn't like this play." It's more dramatic than anything else she's managed. And despite spending nearly six hours on 'We Both Reached For The Gun', the chorus sounds like a flock of deranged cockatoos.

Juliana is run ragged. Her look has morphed from new-age flowerchild to hair-pulling harpie. I've never thought her more attractive. St Seb seems amused as well – he directs more than one swallowed chuckle Juliana's way. Perhaps he isn't quite the sycophant he seems.

Billy Flynn, who appears to be embracing method acting by sleeping his way through the chorus, strides around the stage like he's Kenneth Branagh in *Hamlet*, stopping several times to 'refocus', and at one point complaining, "There's a massive echo in here."

Sebastian rolls his eyes. "Was that echo, or ego?"

Flynn hears and stalks out in a huff. Juliana shoots Seb a betrayed look and scurries after her actor.

I frown at Seb, wondering suddenly, "Why *are* you playing in this poxy school show, if it's not a personal favour to Juliana?"

He shrugs. "Publicity. Research. Kenny never appealed to youth. I'm trying to tap into that lucrative pop/classical crossover market for saxophone. The Vanessa Mae of woodwind." He cracks a grin; a real one this time. It seems that Seb and I have become, if not friends, at least comrades in arms against the maladroit thespians.

When the senior leadership arrive, I feel almost Zen-like: a contrast to Juliana's frantic rodent-like scurrying. The band is calm, electric with energy. I feel almost fond of them.

We begin. I watch, smug, as actors botch their lines, dancers ricochet off each other and the chorus drift aimlessly from scene to scene. The band nails every note. At the finale, our visitors stand and stretch, looking a little shell-shocked. Juliana flutters over to them, beaming. "It's still a little rough, of course, but what did you think?"

The Principal shakes her hand. "Yes, yes, wonderful. Just one question though. Why'd you cut that song? You know the one. 'Chicago, Chicago (That Toddlin' Town)'?"

~

Renée Boyer's Biography

Renée Boyer is a comms manager by day, creative writer at night (and occasionally lunchtime). She lives in beautiful Raglan, New Zealand.

Renée writes prose, poetry and plays, and her 10-minute plays have been performed all over the world, the most recent premiering in Hollywood. She is currently attempting to write a novel, as part of her

Master of Professional Writing at the University of Waikato.

SUPERBOY

Shortlisted story, by Louise Elliman

I am hanging upside-down from the sofa, nearly doing a headstand and looking at my comic at the same time. Clever of me, isn't it? I want Mummy to see but she isn't watching. She's staring at her phone, and scrunching her eyebrows together, like she wants to tell the phone off. She's probably reading the news again.

In my comic, Superboy is smiling at me, daring me to join him. I bet I could run faster than him and get to the park and back before Mummy noticed. She'd be cross if she found out though. Everyone knows baddies are everywhere and one of them might snatch me. Mummy says it's always happening to newspaper children.

I don't know if there's such thing as newspaper children in real life but that doesn't matter. A baddie could never catch up with me, and even if they did, I have this lightsaber. It glows red like a villain's eyes. You'd think it was real if you saw it. I could wave it at a baddie and be all like, "Hyyaa," which would distract them. Then, before they could get out their gun or their child catching net or whatever, I'd be zooming off into the distance like a beam of light from a laser blaster.

"I'm just going in the garden," I say.

"OK, Theo, put your wellies on then," says Mummy without looking at me.

I put my wellies on and monster stomp across the squelchy lawn. Today, I'm a whole superhero team in one seven-year-old boy with my Spider-Man T-shirt, my Hulk wellies and my Batman cape.

The cold air stings my arms like Mr Freeze is trying to zap me. I crouch down and wrap my cape around me. He can't get me down here.

I look up at the sky. It's mostly coloured blue with a few messy clouds splatted up there like exploded snow. That's when I see it. Only one cloud is grey, and it's shaped like a bat. This is a sign. Someone out there is calling for Batman. Every superhero in the land needs to be ready to help.

I look behind me. The kitchen window is covered in a mysterious mist, but I can still see Mummy through it. She is stirring the dinner with one hand and texting with the other. She won't notice if I go invisible for a few minutes.

I crawl through the bushes to our back fence, which is like a giant lolly stick cage. It's easy to climb over and then, before I can think too much, I am running through the fields, past the conker trees, faster and faster, until my breathing swooshes like the wind and then I am the wind, blowing my cape out behind me like a kite. Birds are doing swoopy somersaults above me and now I'm a bird too and I'm not running anymore. I'm flying.

I stop. A road is blocking the way ahead and I'm not allowed to cross roads without Mummy. I think about going home but the bat cloud's still up there. It's changed shape now and flapped over to the other side of the field. I need to investigate. I run across to the big hedge and crawl through. Spiky stones press into my knees all the way until I come out into someone's driveway.

I'm just about to stand up when a long, black car drives up in front of me. I wriggle backwards to hide, and I see a fat man get out. His neck is all squished into his shoulders, his hair's black with grey scribbles in it and he's got a pointy nose like a beak. It's scary to look at him. I put my hands over my face and peep through my fingers. He's not wearing a hat or one of those glasses that goes on one eye but it's still obvious this is Batman's arch enemy – the Penguin.

The Penguin unlocks his front door and shouts, "Hello love, I'm home."

He goes inside. He's left the porch open a bit, so I sneak in and put my ear against the door. I stand still, like a hunter, waiting. I wish I had my lightsaber with me. I wonder if the Penguin's got any weapons.

Inside, I can hear a lady's voice. It sounds squeaky like a little girl but also wobbly like an old person.

"Who are you?" she says. "Where's Malcolm?"

"I am Malcolm, love, remember?"

"You're not my Malcolm. Get off me."

"OK, love, I'm sorry. Oh God."

The Penguin coughs, then says, "I don't know if I can do this. Maybe I should go."

"No, you need to let *me* go," says the lady. "I want to go home. Where are my car keys?"

"You are home, love, and you can't drive. You're not allowed to drive now. The doctor—"

The lady interrupts him, "I can bloody well drive if I want to. Are those my keys in your hand? Have you stolen my car? You're keeping me prisoner here."

I step away from the door. This is worse than I thought. I'd better go home now or else he might make me his prisoner too.

Then the lady shouts, "Right, I'm calling the police, but oh sodding hell, I can't remember their number."

I know the answer to this, and I want the police to rescue her, so before I can stop myself, I push the door open and shout out, "It's 999."

In the living room there is a grey sofa with a lady on it. Her hair is grey, her skin is grey and her clothes are grey. For a second, I think she's been turned into stone, but then she sits up and turns towards me. The Penguin's standing next to her and they're both staring at me like they're expecting me to say something, so I say, "Hello, I'm Theo. I came here by accident. I just wanted to tell you the number you need is 999."

"Why, thank you, Theo," says the grey lady. "Or perhaps I should call you Superboy. Lovely cape you have on."

She reaches for the phone from a shelf beside her and her long bony finger presses the number 9 three times.

"Police please," she says.

Then, before she can say anything else, the Penguin

snatches the phone and throws it behind the sofa. The grey lady tries to get it back, but she can't reach, so she picks up a cushion instead and starts hitting the Penguin with it. He isn't even fighting back. He's just standing there and letting her.

"Help me, Superboy," says Grey Lady, so I grab another cushion.

"KERPOW," I shout as I hit the Penguin's legs. This makes her laugh.

"BOOM," she shouts and bops him on his head.

I leap onto the sofa so that I can reach his head too.

"WHAM, BIFF, BANG," I shout.

Grey Lady's properly giggling now, and we battle together until he finally gives up.

"That's enough now," the Penguin says, then he wraps his fat fingers around Grey Lady's arms and pushes her back down on to the sofa.

At that moment the door opens and a tall policeman with a long face and short police-lady with a round pink face walk in together.

When he hears them, the Penguin pings back up and smooths his hair down with one hand.

"Oh God, they must have traced the call," he says.

The police-lady looks surprised to see me,

"That description we were given, the wellies and the cape?"

"Yep, looks like he fits," says the policeman.

The police-lady kneels down to speak to me. She smells like she's been smoking, which seems like a bad thing the police shouldn't do, but she is smiling and has nice rosy cheeks so I'm pretty sure she's a goodie.

"Are you Theo?" she says, and I nod.

"Theo, your mum's been on the phone to us. She's very worried about you. Are you hurt at all?"

I shake my head.

"OK, Theo, hang on a second, I'll get the station to call your mum."

While the police-lady is on the phone and the policeman's talking to the Penguin, I follow the grey lady into the kitchen. She sits at the table and stares down at her crumply hands.

"These are not my hands," she says, "and this is not my house."

"Don't worry," I tell her, "you'll be safe now. The police are here."

The Penguin's in the other room and he's getting cross.

"Look, young man, you can't arrest me. I'm her husband. Her carer now. I can't just leave her."

I sit down at the table next to the grey lady. There is a biscuit tin in the corner with a picture of swirly chocolate biscuits on it. I wonder if it still has those biscuits in it or if it's been filled with cotton reels or herbs and spices or something. Grown-ups do that to trick children sometimes. I can't decide whether it would be rude to ask her. She turns to look at me, then, and puts her hand on top of mine.

"I hope I never forget you, Superboy," she says.

I open my mouth to talk but that's when the door opens again and this time it's Mummy. She rushes in like a tornado made of tears and snot, squeezes me tightly and keeps saying my name again and again. Then she spots the Penguin walking into the hallway with the policeman.

"You?" she screams, "Did you touch him? Did you? I know all about perverts like you. What did you do? Snatch him from the garden?"

It gets a bit confusing after that, with everyone

shouting at each other. The police are cross with Mummy for coming over, because apparently it was *their* job to bring me home. Mummy is cross with the Penguin, which is good really because it means she's not cross with me, and the Penguin is cross with everybody. I'm pleased when I am finally outside on the driveway with Mummy, watching the policeman handcuffing the Penguin and making sure he is sitting nicely in the police car.

Mummy's thumb is whizzing across her phone. "Just messaging everyone to let them know you're safe."

While I wait, I look back and notice the mysterious mist is on all the windows here too. Grey Lady pushes the kitchen window open so she can see me better and leans out to give me a wave and a smile. I smile back, swish my cape, do a little bow, and just about manage to wave goodbye, before Mummy grabs my arm and drags me away.

~

Louise Elliman's Biography

Louise has been writing short stories for the last two years and is increasingly excited by her new found powers. This year, Louise has won the *Graffiti Magazine* short story competition and has read at Story Sundays in Bristol and at the latest Stroud Short Stories event.

SURVIVING HEELS

Shortlisted story, by Kathryn Joyce

I've almost finished when the phone rings. I ignore it and try to focus on my shavasana, softening my jaw, stilling my eyelids, relaxing my shoulders, seeking balance. They say it's vital at the end of a yoga practice, and the hardest pose to achieve. They're right. Who *was* it, calling me? I roll on my side, sit up, mutter, "Namaste," and stand, bottom first, head last. One day I'll rise as gracefully as the YouTube yogini. Until then,

I'll continue my practice, as they call it, at home.

The missed call was Mellissa. Dan's soon-to-be-bride. I toss the phone on the bed.

The magnifying mirror is unkind – it turns pores into craters, blemishes into age spots, and lines into wrinkles. Unable to decide which is the most effective, I massage vitamin A and rose-hip oil into my face, dab off the excess with a tissue, and swivel the mirror to normal. Greatly improved. I step on the scales, and off, and on again. I sigh.

Finally, I listen to the voicemail. "Hi Charlotte. Just calling about Friday… " The blonde, effervescent voice gushes. "…and so I got us tickets to the nudist festival."

Nudist festival? My mouth dries. I listen again. The hen party is to end at a nudist festival. I feel lightheaded, my body sways, I sit back on the bed. I won't go. I can't go. I'm overweight. I'm 60.

I press call.

"This festival…" I can't say it. "Is everyone going?"

"Sure."

"I thought we were doing afternoon tea, then a couple of pubs."

"We are. Then the festival. Nine o'clock. After dark."

After dark. There's a blessing. "Does Dan know?"

"Dan? Why should he? It's *my* hen party. Anyway, it's not his thing."

"No. I guess not."

It's not mine, either. I turn, breathe in and examine my profile in the mirror. Mellissa's voice continues, explaining where to meet. I open my underwear drawer, rummage amongst greying elastic, close it again.

"So, see you on Friday, then."

I nod. "Four o'clock, Princes Ave. Vintage Café."

Of course, I'm *pleased* that Dan's getting married. It's time. There've been plenty of girls, some of them around for months. Then, three years ago, he met Mellissa. But I'd hoped for better.

A nudist festival? No, no, no.

I take my loose, wide-leg palazzo pants from the wardrobe, and the floating Indian-cotton shirt. And the heels I'd bought years ago when a man I liked had promised me the Earth, then offered camping. Black, strappy, proud, they're survival heels.

I need the heels.

*

A tall, career-type woman stands as I go into the café and moves towards me. "Hi. I'm Annette. You must be Charlotte."

I open my mouth but she turns, heads back to the table. I'm late. But I'm here. I follow.

"Here's Dan's sister." Annette looks at a wall clock. "We're all here, now."

The others smile, shuffle chairs, and Mellissa points. "Guys, this is Charlotte. 'Nette, Jo, Vee, and Simone. We've all…"

"It's Char…*lie*."

Mellissa blinks. Her smile doesn't falter. "Charlie. Yes. Right."

They've unfolded their lace-edged napkins and settled them on skinny leggings, short tight skirts, toned thighs. I shake my napkin, spread it over my palazzos, and pick up the flowered plate in front of me. I turn it over, look at its underside. I want to shake off the heels. Already.

Mellissa giggles. "Can't believe this time next week

I'll be married again."

Amid a chorus of, "About time," and, "Second time lucky," a charm on my bracelet entangles in the embroidered tablecloth. It's the silver fox Dan gave me for my birthday. Dan, who is about to become father to Mellissa's 14 and 12-year-olds. They're already calling me Auntie Charlotte and I don't know how to stop them.

Vee, or is it Jo, says, "Naughty at 40, eh?"

Mellissa squeals, "39."

Laughter. My smile is beginning to feel set.

I look around the table, imagine everyone naked, including me. I shiver, look around the café at tables and chairs my mother might have had, the counter with glass domed cake-stands. Mismatched plates, china cups and saucers, milk-jugs, knitted-tea-cosied teapots clutter tables. Tea? I want a drink.

A waitress wearing a polka dot frock brings plates. Red lips explain the crustless sandwich quarters, savoury pastries and retro stuffed eggs. Then a girl in a dirndl places a huge teapot and a three-tier cake stand. I cringe at mini chocolate eclairs, tiny fruit tarts, pink-iced sponge squares, things my last foster-mother would have called 'fancies' and 'confections'. Tomorrow, I'll fast.

At last, an ice bucket arrives. Everyone cheers as dirndl girl lifts a fat-bottomed bottle. I count six of us and hope there'll be at least another bottle. The cork bursts, glasses fill with bubbles, settle, are topped up and passed round. Annette proposes a toast. "'Lissa," she says. "Wedded bliss." Glasses chink. I sip.

Across the table, Annette holds her glass to her nose. "Glera grape. Buttery, with citrus."

"Nette's a wine buyer." Vee is pushing a plate of

sandwiches at me. "So, you're Dan's sister?"

What sort of a question is that? I take a sandwich. Brown, egg with cress, I think.

"How many of you?"

"Oh, just the two."

A woman and child are passing the window. They stop, look, point at the feast on the table. The boy licks his lips and pats his belly and a fleshy woman – his mother? – blows her cheeks grotesquely. I recall when Dan was young.

Vee's mouth is full of sandwich. "Like us then. Me and my brother. But he's only three years younger."

"Mmm." I ignore the implication and don't explain that 'just the two' meant, literally, just the two of us. I was 17 when Dan was born.

Jo is asking if anyone wants a cup of tea and I'm wishing there was more Prosecco.

"Tea?" Simone waves her empty glass. "Another bottle, I reckon."

I drain my glass.

*

The bar says it's a blues bar. It is, blue floor, blue walls, blue tables and blue seating, but its jazz that hovers. And my shoulders begin to move, though it's not easy when you're squeezed into a leather banquette.

"You like this music?" Simone is tight against me.

I nod, attempt to sway. "Reminds me of jazz clubs I used to go to."

"In Hull?"

"No. In London. At the art college. My boyfriend played trumpet; fancied himself as Dizzie Gillespie." The truth is that I'd worked in the office. I'd said I was 18, had passed some exams. I'd had enough of school, foster parents, social services by then.

"Dizzie who?"

I stir my mojito. "American, 60s. Latin, jazz, bebop. He played with a bent trumpet because he liked the sound. My boyfriend bent his trumpet so he could play like his hero."

"Did it work?"

"Nah."

We laugh together and I wonder if Simone is as relaxed as she appears to be.

"And the boyfriend?"

I suck the minty toothpaste-tasting cocktail up a straw. "Didn't work either. Daddy was an American diplomat. Took his boy home." I sing, "Bye bye love..."

"Bye bye happiness?"

"Life moved on."

"And you got on with being an artist?"

"No. Didn't work out either."

*

"Sorry. Sorry." I stumble, trying to share Vee's umbrella. The rest have run on, out of the rain. Ridiculous heels.

We shoulder our way into the crowded, noisy pub where the others are. There are no seats.

"There y'go, Charlo... Charlie." Mellissa hands me a glass. "Enjoying...?"

"Sorry?"

Mellissa raises her voice. "Enjoying yourself?"

"Oh. Yes. Sure. Lovely. Nice you asked me..."

"Well, we'll be family soon, me and you."

"Sorry?"

"Family. Soon. Me. You." She's waving her glass.

I raise mine too. "Cheers."

Jo is saying we should go to another bar – one where she knows the owners.

*

The air is cooler outside, summer damp after the rain. We pass a gaggle of girls, all hair, half-dresses, and heels twice the height of my own. Friday night revellers on a Princes Avenue big night out. Another hen-party? They might love this nudist festival. I picture myself at home.

*

Jo cheek-kisses a barman who nods and indicates the wide, uneven stairs. I hold the handrail and follow the others. Mellissa finds a table and pushes dirty glasses aside.

The barman brings a tray of glasses and a bottle of red wine.

"Girls' night out?" He's collecting used glasses.

"'Lissa's hen party." Jo passes fresh glasses.

The barman winks at Mellissa. "Another one gone."

Jo laughs, points at Simone and Vee, "Another one gone, another one gone..."

Then they're all Freddie Mercury, belting out, 'Another One Bites the Dust' into make-believe microphones.

Except Annette, who swirls red wine, holds it to the light then to her nose. She inhales. "Good colour, extended notes of pepper. And dark cherry." She sips. "Bold to begin, then softer, spicy."

I cringe into my glass. Tannin coats my tongue.

Vee announces, "Last drink, then on to the festival."

My heart skips, my stomach contracts. I'm waiting for someone to say it's a joke. All a joke. I ask Vee, casually, "You been to this sort of thing before?" Why can't I say it?

"Sure." Vee waves a hand. "'Lissa, Jo. We went last year. Loved it."

"Oh?" I glance at Mellissa and wish I was surprised. "Do you think there'll be, well, a lot of people there?"

"Oh, loads. 'Lissa got cancellations. There's a huge stage – I saw it from the bus."

"Outside? Will it be warm enough?"

"It will be when we get dancing."

Dancing? I excuse myself, head for the Ladies.

The mirror, crazed with age, reflects my outfit. It's flopping more than flowing. My feet, crippled in their swaddling, are swollen. I want, more than anything, to go home.

They're standing as I return. I avoid their eyes, I'm searching for a way to say I've decided to go home.

Feeling sick?

Migraine?

I need a reason, not an excuse.

I head down the stairs, pause half-way to see if they're following, and my heel twists. I grab but miss the handrail. My ankle turns, my knee is forced sideways, I'm falling, backwards, against the stairs and momentum takes me. Something crunches my hip. I'm bumping, ridge over ridge, sliding, until I lie, gratefully prostrate, at the bottom of the stairs. It's over. Relief is like an incoming tide, rolling, enveloping me.

There's noise; shouting, feet banging on the stairs. There's pain. A blade pierces my knee, needles stab my ankle, a drill bores my hip. But I've stopped falling so all is wonderful. Faces appear, mouths move, hands reach, confusion buzzes. This, I think, might be death, and I give it permission to take me away.

"Charlotte."

Someone is lifting my shoulders, something soft is being placed under my head.

"Charlie. Wake up. Please wake up. Dan'll never..."

Someone is fussing with my clothes. I open my eyes.

"Oh, thank God."

Thank God, indeed. I have found my reason. "I think I'd better go home."

"Home? An ambulance..."

They're concerned, caring. It takes time to convince them I'm not hurt. Not badly enough for an ambulance, anyway.

"Just a taxi."

Fortunately, they still want to have fun.

*

Paracetamol, ibuprofen, and coffee carry me to the next day when, around 10, I hear Dan's key in the lock.

I'm on the sofa, my right leg resting on cushions with a bag of frozen peas alternating between blackening ankle and ballooning knee.

Dan stands in front of me with a bunch of sunflowers and his *you-should-have-known-better* raised eyebrow. "Nothing broken, then?"

"No."

"The flowers are from the pub. 'Liss says you were lucky. Apparently, you were well anaesthetised." The green of his eyes are dark so I know he's more concerned than critical.

"Well, it's probably as well. Who knows what'd have happened if I hadn't had a few glasses?" I wince, mostly for effect.

"You probably wouldn't have fallen."

"It was the heels."

He does the eyebrow raise again. At-*your-age*? He doesn't understand heels.

"Shame you didn't make the festival. You used to like Bryan Adams."

"Bryan Adams?" I'd tried, failed to get tickets. I'd told Mellissa...

"At the music festival..."

"Music festival?" Laughter gurgles in my belly, rattles the ache in my hip. I hug myself as it froths, erupts. "Music." I rock, guffaw, tears begin to fall.

Dan kneels, takes my hands. "Hey, sis. You OK?"

Sis.

Things are different now. Nobody cares. They did then. I brought my baby back to Hull and lies became our truths.

I touch Dan's face. He's older, but there's still a look of his father. It's the eyes I remember the most, the green irises that changed colour when he was anxious or amused. Or amorous.

"Sit down, Dan. I've got something to tell you." I shift aside, pat the sofa, and tell myself it's time to ditch the heels.

~

Kathryn Joyce's Biography

Kathryn Joyce (Kathy) began writing fiction for the second time in 2009 when she returned from a year spent working in Lahore, Pakistan. (Her first-time-writing began at an early age but slowed up as life gathered pace. Somewhere, amongst the detritus of her loft, ghostly scribbles, riddles and rhymes lie rotting in boxes.) Then, on a damp day somewhere in Peterborough, she asked of a friend, "What next?" The friend, who claimed to have enjoyed newsletters Kathy sent home from Pakistan and elsewhere, suggested she write a book.

The debut novel, *Thicker Than Soup*, is a story of a British Pakistani girl who travels, in curiosity, to Pakistan. It was published in 2015. Since then, Kathy has devoted her skills to writing short fiction. "I enjoy telling lies," she explains. "There are so many of them."

Born in Hull, Kathy has lived and written unexcitingly in more than 60 countries where she has worked or travelled. Recently retired, she now writes simply for the pleasure of crafting words. With stories shortlisted in Eyelands International Short Story Contest and published by Strange Days Books, she continues to write about the vagaries of life from downtown Lincolnshire.

THE BIRTH OF GOD

Shortlisted story, by Rob McInroy

In an ordinary green field, in middle England, a cow surveyed its surroundings and wondered whether there should be more to life. The grass in the neighbouring field looked a delicious shade of green, rich and vibrant, evidently full of nutrients. For the past week, her daydreams had been filled with the vicarious delights of eating that grass. That must be, she had thought, the acme of experience. She slowly chewed on air, pretending the virgin grass was on her tongue, between her teeth, sliding down her throat into her rumen, there to soften up before passing into her reticulum, omasum and abomasum.

But now she wasn't so sure. What if it was a trick of the light? What if that grass wasn't all she imagined it do be? What if – and this was highly likely, the more she thought about it – what if beyond that field there was another field with even richer, greener grass? And beyond that another one? And yet another one? It was too much to contemplate. She might walk two miles in search of the perfect grass and never find it. And what if it was here all along, beneath her hooves, only she wasn't intelligent or cultivated or educated enough to recognise it?

Then, in confusion and growing distress, she began to wonder whether the quest for perfect grass should be the summit of her ambition anyway? Couldn't she aspire to something grander than the consumption of monocotyledonous plant life? Was this as good as it got? So began the cow's existential crisis.

At first, no one noticed. A morose cow is barely distinguishable from a happy one, even for other cows. And so she kept herself to herself, standing alone beneath the shade of an ageing chestnut tree which, the more she contemplated it, became less and less substantial. Finally, convinced that it was a figment of her imagination, she ran into it full pelt and was concussed for a week. By the time she recovered, she had forgotten what had caused her headaches and began, anew, to ponder the reality of the tree and the significance of things. She walked around it clockwise and then again, anti-clockwise, following the twist and curve of its trunk, memorising the texture of its bark until, through a form of self-hypnosis, she became convinced that she was the tree and the tree was a cow. At this point, the herd began to perceive a change in her but, not being versed in the techniques of cognitive behaviour therapy, they failed to offer her the community support that might have saved her life.

She became paranoid that her roots were coming adrift and she would surely crash to the ground in the next puff of wind. Tentatively, she lifted one leg after the other and imagined herself teetering from side to side. In desperation, she tried to dig herself into the ground, selecting – intelligently enough for a cow, or even a tree for that matter – the boggier ground at the foot of the field, nearest the river. Time and again, she reared up and planted her front legs into the muddy soil, churning it up and softening it until, finally, she was buried to her fetlocks. Then she shook her rump from side to side in an attempt to force her hind legs downwards. The herd watched with dispassion as she slowly, carefully, lovingly, rooted herself in the fine English soil.

When she was satisfied, she stood stock-still, waiting for a wind to blow and test her solidity. The thought of spring, only weeks away, was exciting her: all those new shoots budding, growing, life from life, stretching into the sky in hopeful tendrils. For the first time, she felt she had a purpose, she felt valuable. Look at that cow, she thought, staring contemptuously at the chestnut tree, all it does is eat and fart. It's methane on legs. She, on the other hand, noble English chestnut, she turned carbon dioxide into oxygen. The mere fact of her existence, planted in the soil, was helping to save the world.

Yes, she thought, she was saving the world, she was

the saviour of the planet. Without her, doom was inevitable. Only she stood between the Earth and catastrophe. The corollary was clear: she must be God. She must be the divine imagination which had conjured grass and clover, invented bone meal, designed country lanes, milking maids, pails. She alone had seen that the Earth was nothing but a void, empty and dark, and she became the sun in the morning and the rain in the evening, she was the wind that blew and the grass that grew. She brought forth every living creature, the cattle and creeping things and beasts of the Earth, according to their kinds. Cows and sheep, dogs, rabbits, humans even. And she saw these things. And she saw that it was good.

And with that thought, a hideous weight fell upon the cow who became the tree that was revealed to be God. All that responsibility, the knowledge that the future of every living being – and there must be hundreds of them – rested with her, and her alone. It was the most solitary burden in the world, but she would bear it with fortitude, because the world required it of her. All of this I have made from the slime of the Earth, she thought, and in that reckoning she became aware of her own substance, the mighty chestnut, the lord of all she surveyed. All of these things she had created – she looked at them with a mixture of beneficence and aloofness – should they not now bow at her hooves and give thanks to her, their God, for making them, nourishing them, letting them live amid her bountiful splendour?

Yea, she thought, the world should bear witness to her munificent gifts. It would have to learn to appreciate her. And her heart grew hard, because were there not those who would repel her, refuse to acknowledge her power? Any who cherished her name and denied not her faith, they would surely be blessed, but all others dwelt with evil.

She would have to establish rules, certainties. After all, even she hadn't realised she was God, so how could the rest of the world know? How could she make them understand that she, God, required their worship? That she expected from them blind devotion, adoration, treats? She would have to proclaim herself Mistress of every field between here and there, the right and true owner of every drop of water that had ever been and every inch of soil in which her pure and virtuous roots now stretched. It was a huge job for one soul. She would have to be everywhere at once, a simultaneous entity. Again, inspiration struck: she would have to learn how to fly.

Trembling with fear at the revelation of her righteous destiny, she tried to ponder the nature of flight but, without an understanding of the laws of gravity, she was at more of a disadvantage than she realised. Nonetheless, she observed her front legs, buried six inches into the ground and knew instinctively that this was not a good position from which to start. She began to rock from side to side while the herd mooed their encouragement, settling at once into a laconic, steady rhythm. She regarded the cows disparagingly. Dumb creatures, they knew so little of the world around them. They were concerned with nothing grander than the search for fresh, green grass, while she, God, had the future of everything thrust on her quivering haunches.

Thus it was, in deep contemplation, that she failed to notice that her rocking, far from releasing her from the mud, was sinking her ever deeper into it. She planned an amnesty for rabbits as long as they promised no longer to eat grass reserved for the cows. She pondered how best to eradicate the fox, what to do with the badger, how to ensure humans stopped slapping cows on the rump in that indelicate and unnecessary manner. She planned grand, chestnut-based rituals to celebrate her glory. Her stomach became stuck in the ground as she worded a decree banishing, with immediate effect, flies and midges to a field without grass at least four miles away, on the other side of the river. The buzzing things hadn't been one of her best inventions, she now conceded. Her shoulder blades slid under the soil, and her back and her rump, too, leaving only her neck and head free. Still she didn't notice, busy as she was preparing an ordinance on the offsetting of cow-methane with tree oxygen which would require the number of cows and the number of trees to be maintained in perfect symmetry.

Momentum was driving her down, the ground by now so loosened she was sinking fast. Her nose tickled as soil settled around it. Her eyes began to stream, her lungs to burn. This must be some form of rapture, she supposed, reserved only for the supreme God. She was privileged to experience it. The light around her was dimming, a soft English breeze fanning her last remaining visible portions. In the distance she could hear the bucolic mooing of cows, the soft rustle of trees in the evening. This is all very pleasant, she thought, her soul detaching, drifting, rising effortlessly into the sky. She looked down on the tranquil scene, the cows chewing peaceably, rabbits scampering, foxes prowling. She noticed the greenness of adjacent fields, deepest emerald, shimmering. At the bottom of the near most field, next to the river, she saw the strangest sight. Silly thing, she thought, there's a cow there that thinks it's a rabbit. But already she was floating, far, far away from such minor concerns, a hundred miles or even more. She had a planet to save, subjects to attend to. Is this what it's like to be God, she wondered. And then she wondered no more.

~

Rob McInroy's Biography

Rob McInroy has won four short story competitions in the past year (Hissac, ChipLit Fest, *Writing Magazine* and the Bedford International Writing Competition). His short stories have been placed or shortlisted in a further 16 competitions in the past 18 months. In 2018, he was a winner of the Bradford Literature Festival Northern Noir Crime Novel competition with *Cuddies Strip*, a novel based on a true crime in 1930s Scotland.

THE RUNNING MAN

Shortlisted story, by Pat Winslow

When the alarm starts, people open their doors and look at each other. "Is it real," they ask. They laugh and talk as they head towards the fire exit. No one is running. There are no shouts. He goes back in to get his book. He was half-way through the last chapter when the alarm started. It always happens like this, he thinks. Just when you get near the end, someone phones or knocks at the door.

The alarm stops suddenly. He wonders whether to just stay and read, but he tucks his book in his jacket pocket and closes the door softly behind him.

He came up in the lift, so he has no idea where the stairs are. In case of fire, do not use lift, he remembers. He presses the button anyway. Nothing happens. The electric's off. He carries on down the corridor and goes through two sets of double doors. Follow the signs, the white man on the green background. Take note which way the arrow is pointing. Straight ahead and two lefts. He passes a cleaning trolley that smells vaguely of polish and oranges. Where have they gone? he wonders. Surely he must pass someone soon. He stops and listens. He goes through another set of double doors. The white man is pointing left again.

Another set of double doors. He pushes them open and stops. The white man is still pointing left. He's back where he started. Six doors down is his room. He must have missed the stairs. He should have been looking. In some buildings the white man is green on a fire door. He's silhouetted against a white oblong. He doesn't walk, either. He runs. He's always running. The running man doesn't bother following rules. He gets to the nearest exit and keeps going 'til he's outside.

Past his room then, through the two sets of double doors, checking all the single doors on the way, following the running man and the arrow, straight ahead and two lefts, past the cleaning trolley again. Ah, the white man isn't pointing left. He misread it. The white man is pointing *diagonally* left. There's a small step leading to a window with an empty vase on the sill. The fire door is tucked to the side. No wonder he missed it. And the white man has turned green. The green man is running into an oblong of white.

He pushes the door open and finds himself in a stairwell. He looks up. There are three floors above him.

He looks down and counts four below. There's a round emergency light on the wall but it's not working. The only source of light is the glass panel in the roof. He detects the smell of rubberised safety treads. He feels strangely comforted by this.

Down then, smartly. He doesn't bother to look at the running man because the ground floor is where he wants to be, past reception, through the automatic doors and out finally into the carpark with everyone else standing around talking in the sun or on their phones, and a fire fighter striding over saying everything's been checked, a false alarm, you can all go back in now.

At the bottom, the running man has changed colour again. He's going into a green oblong. He pushes the door open and finds another corridor like the one he's just left. He looks for the sign. There are two. One behind him and one in front. It doesn't matter which one he chooses. Both directions lead to a safe place. He goes forward, comes to a double door, goes through and turns left. He expects to see service rooms and a lounge, then reception. Instead, he sees a pair of brown leather shoes outside a door and, further on, a metal clothes rack filled with clothes hangers. He goes left through another set of double doors. There are just two doors in this corridor. One of them is open. He can't help glancing through as he goes past. What he sees makes him gasp. Behind the large polished desk with the computer is the city's skyline. How is it possible that he's at the top of the building? He's just gone down four flights of stairs.

There's a balcony. The window is a sliding door. He goes over and tries it. It's locked. He thinks he sees the air thickening around him, that the corners of the room are becoming blurred and indistinct, that something is curling down through the air vent. He leaves. He runs through the doors at the end, follows the sign to the left and finds the fire door. He opens it. Seven floors down. He checks first. Looks up. Nothing. To the ground this time and then out.

At the bottom, he finds the white man turned green, pushes the door and goes through. He's back where the signs face two directions at once. He's back on the top floor. This time, he follows the running man behind him. He turns right and right again and there's the same dry-cleaning rack and the same pair of brown leather shoes. Try a different stairwell, he thinks. He pushes each door he runs past. Finally, he finds one on the right with a green man. He goes through.

The stairwell is filled with sunlight. There are windows on each landing. He looks down and counts the handrails. Eight, not seven. Eight? Of course. He's been forgetting to count the floor he's standing on. Eight means the last one he can see is the ground floor. If he looks through each window as he descends, he'll see the city. He'll see whether he's going up or down. It's not possible to be going up when you're going down, but he knows there are roads that do that. A famous one in Scotland. You can freewheel up it if you have a bicycle. It's all to do with the lie of the land.

On the seventh floor he looks out. He can see the business district. He can see planes flying low towards the airport. The afternoon sun is strong. The windows don't open. No chance of escape that way. In any case, who could get a ladder up this high? Unless they had one of those turntable things.

It's getting hotter. If the fire is above, the floors will be hot. They might fall through at some point. He takes off his tie and stuffs it in his pocket. On the sixth landing, he takes off his jacket and unbuttons his shirt. He can see over the street to the building opposite. There's a big open-plan office. No one is looking across. A woman with a ponytail has her back to him. She's waving a sheet of paper around. If there was a fire, wouldn't they all be staring out of the windows watching what was going on?

Fifth landing. Fourth. He's rolled his cuffs up now. Is the building really getting hotter? Maybe the fire is below. That's why the smoke was rising through the air vents. He could be running into a trap. He looks out through the window and is shocked to discover that the office block has become apartments. Each window has a different set of blinds or curtains. Some of the windows are open, some are closed. A man is yawning and looking out. He waves to him and realises he must do something larger to attract his attention, so he takes off his shirt and swings it about above his head. The man sees him. He drops his shirt and mimes holding a phone to his ear then points at the man. "You phone," he mouths. "I am trapped." The man looks away. He picks up his shirt again and starts waving it frantically. He takes off one of his shoes and smacks it against the window. It's double glazed, toughened, and nothing happens. The man has gone, anyway. He puts his shoe back on and continues down the stairwell.

"It's hot because the air conditioning's off," he says to himself. "I'm hot because I'm scared and the sun's out and I've been running. Sit down. You're not thinking straight. No one's looking out of the windows. There is no fire. You're going up when you should be going down and the building opposite keeps changing. You're panicking. It's the one thing you shouldn't do."

When he's calmer, he levers himself up to look through the window. It's not apartments and it's not an office block. It's the second floor of a department store. This is ridiculous. There's an escalator running up past the windows from below. He can see people moving along it. How can a building keep changing? He runs down to the next floor. He can see the street. He can see the road he drove up and the sign for the carpark at the back.

He realises he's left his shirt and jacket on the landing overlooking the apartments. He decides not to go back for them in case he gets lost again. He wonders how he'll seem standing bare-chested in his shoes and trousers. He should wipe the sweat off at least. He should push his hair back and run his fingers through it a couple of times. He has a tissue in his pocket. He passes it over his face and chest and wipes the insides of his hands. He sleeks his hair back. When he gets to the ground floor, he pushes open the door and finds himself in a corridor with a waste bin and a water cooler. He balls the tissue up and puts it back in his pocket, then he pours himself a cup of cold water and drinks it slowly. He pours another one.

He realises he's standing outside the lift and notices the power's back on, that the lights are working on the request buttons. He drinks the second cup of water quickly, tosses it into the bin and walks towards the double doors at the end of the corridor. He can hear a phone. The lobby is straight ahead. A phone means everything is back to normal. He pushes open the doors and strides through. He puts his hands in his pockets. Look like you were just about to get in the shower when this happened. Look like you took your time about coming down to see what all the fuss was about. He lengthens his stride. The phone is still ringing. One more set of double doors. He opens them, turns right and sees the executive office at the top of the building again. The water rises into his mouth and he swallows it back down. The phone's still ringing. He goes over to the desk and picks up the receiver. Too late. Whoever it was has hung up. He puts the phone back. Wearily, he sits down in the soft leather chair and swivels around in it a few times. He looks out across the city at the planes.

When he turns in again, he notices a key on the desk. He picks it up and goes over to the balcony window, fits it into the lock and slides the window open. The air is hot and humid. He takes in the sound of the city below. He stretches, scratches his chest, goes back in and closes the window. He feels calmer now. He picks up the phone. What is it usually in these places to get the lobby? 1 or 0. He tries both. Nothing. He tries every number. 9 gets him an outside line. He dials home. No one's picking up. They're all out. Shopping probably. They've found a shady awning to sit under to have cakes and ice cream. He tries her mobile. Nothing.

Eventually, he decides to go back to his room. He picks up his shirt and jacket on the fourth floor, checks his key card is still in the pocket, climbs the stairs to level five and goes in and puts the book on his bed. He strips off and has a shower. He shaves, puts aftershave on, moisturises his face and hands. He combs his hair and selects a fresh shirt from his case. He gets dressed again and lies with his bare feet up on the bed reading the final chapter of his book. He changes his mind and flicks on the TV. He switches on the kettle in the corner of the room and opens up the little catering packet of biscuits. He empties a tube of coffee into the cup and pours hot water into it. He stirs creamer in. He lies back on the bed and flicks from channel to channel. Soap, adverts, old TV series, racing, music channels, 24 hour rolling news. He watches the news, half expects to see his building on it. It's just the usual round of crime and politics and celebrity weddings. He turns the TV off and goes back to his book.

A noise outside his window distracts him on the last page. He looks up. There are two men, one in a white boiler suit and one in green, washing and wiping the glass.

"Hey," he shouts.

They don't see him.

He bangs on the glass. The man in green looks at him.

"How do you open this window?" he asks him.

"You can't," the man in green mouths. "Safety."

He presses a button and the cleaning cradle starts to go up.

"Wait."

But the cradle's gone.

He runs into the corridor. This time he tries the lift. He jabs the button. The lift is stuck on G. He runs two at a time up the stairs. On the seventh landing he has to stop. He has a stitch. It bends him double. He runs up the last flight, hurls himself through the door and runs into the executive office just in time to see the cradle going back down. He grabs the key from the table and opens the sliding window.

"Hey," he calls. "Come back."

The green man and the white man look up at him.

"Come back," he calls again. "I can't get out. I'm trapped."

They look away and the cradle continues on down.

"Come back."

He throws his book at them, aiming to hit them, but the book bounces off the ledge below and the cover detaches. He watches as the book spins and the pages start to tear away from the spine. One page comes free and sways and flutters and gets caught in a sudden updraft. The rest of the book disappears. That'll be the last page, he thinks, and he sinks to the floor remembering the coffee he's left behind and the key card which is sitting on the bedside cabinet next to his mobile.

~

Pat Winslow's Biography

Pat Winslow worked for 12 years as an actor before leaving the theatre in 1987. She has published seven poetry collections, most recently, *Kissing Bones*, from Templar Poetry.

Pat collaborated with composer Oliver Vibrans on her version of 'The Coat', a folk tale from the Caucasus, for the Royal College of Music earlier this year. She frequently works with Oxford Concert Party both in performance and as a workshop facilitator in day centres and schools, and she is part of a group of poets and artists from Oxford and Bonn which enjoys a rich cultural exchange.

For more information see: www.patwinslow.com

Pat also blogs at: www.thepatwinslow.blogspot.co.uk

WITH LOVES AND HATES AND PASSIONS JUST LIKE MINE

Shortlisted story, by Ian Tucker

I saw her first. One of those dreaded sunny days which are bright like summer but they tell me are cold to be out in. The cemetery gates were closed, so she squeezed in past the loose fence panel. There was no shoving or prodding or investigation, so she'd done it before, although I must have missed her when she had. Probably at night then, when they make me sleep. I thought of her as Joyce.

A big bottomed girl, black leather clothing and china white skin. They make the rocking world go 'round, such girls, whether they are happy about it or not. She inspected a few gravestones and scribbled some inscriptions in a notebook, then heffalumped down the path, like a death-cult Moomin on a fieldtrip. It's like Rosencrantz and Guildenstern for me, that path. I assume the graveyard continues beyond the sight lines from my window, but do I really know?

She didn't return before they came to pull the curtains for me at dusk. Another incomplete story.

Him, I saw after. Like the appearance of an electron that you know must exist because you've found a proton, or the inevitable yang for every yin. Oh, I know my philosophy and my science – I've a lot of time for reading. Most of it's pointless. I thought of him as Mike.

He was a weed and, like many weeds, had grown tall. Poor, I'd say, with a denim jacket that didn't fit or suit him, a big nose and an overbite I could see from my second-floor window. Nothing wrong with my eyes, even if I can't hold binoculars to them. He wore bottle glasses. I had a laugh at that.

I could tell what he was like. He was sensitive and clumsy and bewildered and bright and thought of himself as a poet, but really only understood song lyrics. How did I know that? No idea. Is it true if I'm certain in my own mind and no one ever proves me wrong? It is, at least, true 'for me', and that should be enough. I can't remember who said that and haven't the energy to talk to the internet. And, anyway, the words you use should be your own, you shouldn't plagiarise or take 'on loan'.

Joyce passed him on the path while he was reading something carved on a pointy obelisk, which some

Victorian thought would guarantee the perpetuity of his fame, or at least his name. Perhaps the tomb was one of her favourites. Perhaps she liked weeds. Perhaps she was just lonely. Anyway, she spoke to him. They didn't look at each other, only at the monument, but they took a long time to discuss whatever is written there. It made me wonder what it could say that was so fascinating. They must be fine phrases indeed. Maybe Keats or Yates or Wilde or Morrissey.

I could ask one of the people who come to change my bags if they would go out and take a look, but they would probably just laugh. They tell me I have a sense of humour. And, anyway, the cemetery gates are 50 or 60 metres down the road, so such an outing would be a hardship I couldn't, in all conscience, inflict upon them.

After that, the pair came quite often, all through that long summer. Or at least, I remember it being long. That's what you say about summers of the past, isn't it? Good things used to have more duration regardless of what it might say in the contemporary meteorological reports.

They rarely arrived together. Usually, one would dither on the path, always within range of the obelisk, like it was some kind of anchor to which they were tethered. Then, when the other appeared, they'd act nonchalant as if it was all just another coincidence. There wasn't a specific time of day, so text messages or WhatsApp's or emails must have been going on in the background world I cannot see from my window. I guessed it was written communication. They didn't seem the type to be glued to long phone calls although, unlike so many people, they did talk. They never touched.

A few times, they were already there in the morning

when I was wheeled to the window, 'where I like to be', and the curtains were opened. At least once, they were there at dawn sitting with their backs to headstones, drinking from cans and smoking. Some people wouldn't like that. But they always took their rubbish away.

Mike filled out during that summer. By the time the back to school adverts were appearing on TV, he almost fitted his jacket. He also slouched less. On Joyce's part, her face became brown and freckly, and on the hottest days she wore a patterned skirt above her boots. It didn't suit her any more than Mike's jacket suited him.

I wondered if I could have fancied him when I was younger. Not really. I'd always yearned after rippling muscles and jutting jawlines. We value what we cannot get. But then, she wasn't my ideal either. I'd have wanted to be something slimmer and more prone to skip. They weren't like me. But then, I enjoy watching the birds and the bats and the foxes that roam the graveyard when the people are gone, and none of them are like me either. Few things in nature are like me. They'd be easy prey if they were.

The climactic day came in early autumn. Mike was there first, gravely reading the stones of all those people, all those lives while I watched him and thought about how my body was better than any who had lived and died and were buried beneath that earth. He seemed to envy them in a way I could not.

Two tattooed men came up the path from the part of the graveyard that may or may not exist. They were not like Mike. Although he had a tattoo, his was not on his shaved head. And did I mention he was black? They were not.

They stopped by him and aped about. The mute show from my window was easy to understand even before Rosencrantz grabbed Mike's woven bag and flung it into the brambles, before Guildenstern shoved him to the ground and before the pair swaggered off up the hill to the gates, laughing like cartoon hyenas.

Joyce was standing at the gates watching Mike and the approaching men.

He saw her. She knew he'd seen her.

She turned and ran away before Rosencrantz and Guildenstern reached her.

After that, I didn't see Mike again. Occasionally, I saw Joyce, on her own, looking at the stones.

The last time was late in the year, when it was too dark and cold to expect anyone to be out, but she was there one morning sitting with her back to a headstone drinking from a can and smoking. There were a lot of empties and she had a china white face again, although some of the makeup had run. She stayed a long time and stumbled on the path on the way out. She still took her rubbish with her.

If they had come to me, I would have told them never to be ashamed of weakness. But they didn't come and I cannot seek them out. Which makes me wonder what such advice can be worth if I am too weak to deliver it? Even if it might make all the difference to a man and a woman with loves and hates and passions just like mine.

~

Ian Tucker's Biography

Ian writes largely for his own fun when time permits. Such outputs as are put out largely involve whodunit crime, light horror and dry humour. They would end up on www.tilebury.com if he could remember how to add additional content.

The pinnacle of his life has involved being short and longlisted in previous To Hull And Backs.

He lives in Bristol with wife and woodlice. The spiders have largely moved on to a posher house.

JUDGES' STORIES

A GIFT FOR GRANDMA

Judge's story, by Thomas David Parker

I always found it difficult to get a gift for my grandma when I was young. This was mainly due to the fact she was a witch. I do not mean this in a metaphorical sense, although she wasn't particularly pleasant, but that she was a genuine pagan ritual practicing, bought all her clothes in Glastonbury, full member of the occult. And let me tell you, witches are not easy to buy for.

Now, they read a lot, but aren't really the type to use a Waterstones' gift card. They like the outdoors but are unlikely to be needing a new Gore-Tex jacket. And their diet is weird; it's hard to find the stuff they like, even in Holland and Barratt. What I'm saying is, buying her gifts was tricky. If you'll pardon the pun.

This all changed when I was 12 and accidentally gave her one of her favourite gifts of all time. I was at the age where I had begun rebelling against my parents, spent most of my time on my computer and found the real world an inconvenience. So, having my mother tell me we had to visit Grandma was hugely annoying. That it was her birthday and I had to bring a present was doubly so. I protested that buying her something was an impossible task and that I had already made plans with my friend, Ben, but my mother insisted I had to go. I explained that I didn't have time to buy Grandma a present and it would be better to stay home than arrive empty-handed. Her response was to simply state that she had meant to remind me to buy something sooner, and just because she forgot was no excuse for me not to go. This was one of those nonsensical arguments that were impossible to counter, but then my mother had always possessed a supernatural ability to persuade people with non-logical arguments. I guess it must be one of the powers she inherited as the daughter of a witch.

So, we went, under the provision that her present was a joint gift from both of us and that she agreed that Ben could come along. I thought it might be a tough sell to convince him that visiting an old lady was better than an evening playing video games, but he seemed quite keen. He'd never met a witch before and had lots of questions. What I failed to realise at the time, was just how awkward his questions would become.

"Did you go to Hogwarts?" he asked, as soon as we got through the door.

"Where's your pointy hat? How many warts do you have? Do you really fly on a broomstick?"

My mother and I stood there in an embarrassed silence. We don't like talking about the family's magical side, mainly because the rest of us are non-practising, but also because there's always been an unspoken understanding that it's not very polite to question someone on their beliefs.

My grandma just smiled and leaned forward in her seat, gesturing for him to come closer so she could confide her secrets. When he approached, she tapped him on the head with her finger and said a word (that for your own safety I won't repeat here) and he began to shrink. I leapt up in protest, but my mother grabbed my arm and gave me a look to show I shouldn't intervene. Instead, I watched in stunned silence as my friend became smaller and smaller, and hairier, until all that was left was a pile of clothes and a very confused looking black terrier.

"Thank you for my gift," my grandma said. "Very kind." And with that, she picked up the dog and started petting it in her lap. Soon after, my mother hurried me out of the door and took me home.

"What's going to happen to Ben?" I asked, once we were safely in the car.

"He'll stay with Grandma now," my mother replied.

"Will she change him back?"

"She didn't change your Uncle Roger back, so I doubt it."

I didn't remember having an Uncle Roger, but I remembered Grandma having a goldfish called Roger.

And with that memory and my mother's stern tone, I decided to drop it.

Suffice to say, if you ever see an elderly woman with bohemian clothes, erratic hair, and a small and very well behaved black dog, it's probably best to be very polite and keep out of her way.

~

Thomas David Parker's Biography

Thomas David Parker was born in Bristol, but was quickly exiled to the Forest of Dean so his childhood could be shaped into an Enid Blyton novel. From a young age, he discovered a joy of stories and was drawn to the realms of fantasy and the supernatural. His earliest influence was Terry Pratchett, but later joined by Neil Gaiman and M. R. James.

He currently lives above a greengrocer with an ill-tempered snake and an even more ill-tempered flatmate. He likes to say he shoots people in the face for a living, as it sounds far more dramatic than portrait photographer. He has published several short stories, performed a sell-out show at the Edinburgh Fringe, and is constantly planning more creative projects. He is a member of Stokes Croft Writers and co-host of Talking Tales, a bi-monthly YouTube/Bristol based storytelling event.

Twitter: @tomshotphoto

~

Tom's Competition Judging Comments

Wow, what a year. In a world where madness reigns supreme and life is stranger than fiction, it's a joy to escape into the worlds created by the shortlisted writers. Some are clearly destined for professional success and others destined for professional help. Inevitably, some are destined for both.

Christopher Fielden requested that I rank these stories in order of preference, a near-impossible task that caused me to curse his name more than once and invent some new blasphemies that I wrote down for later. However, it is also a privilege to be able to champion some of these stories and I'm grateful for the opportunity to read them. As much as I tried to tie as many stories as I could, Christopher is a tough taskmaster and stood firm until I was forced to choose.

The winning story is a well-deserved winner, but I'm sure you'll agree there are some corkers in the runners up. I hope you've enjoyed reading the stories far more than I did ranking them.

Until next time, I'm off for a lie-down.

C.R.A.P.

Judge's story, by Mark Rutterford

I suffer from a disorder. It's quite a specific disorder. Rare.

I have triggering events and immediate, extreme symptoms.

I've had it happen to me at all sorts of times, in all sorts of places... with all sorts of people.

It might happen with you.

My condition, my disorder... is emotional. It's

behavioural. And it's so rare and so specific, the medical profession – the psychological, psycho-therapeutic, head-doctoring branch of the medical profession – haven't even named it yet.

I've named it for them – they'll catch up in time.

It is compulsive, it is repetitive, it is amorous... that detail is worrying you, because I've already said it might happen with you. You'll be nervous of meeting me now. Wondering if I will shake your hand in the first minute and then shag your leg like a randy Yorkshire Terrier in the next – all done so quickly that you didn't even notice.

Distasteful – certainly.

Messy – probably.

I can imagine you now, surreptitiously looking at your shins thinking of the... residue.

Relax.

I haven't shagged anyone's lower leg. Not in a while, anyway. If I did it with you, it would only be for a laugh.

My condition, my disorder – I've called it C.R.A.P.

Compulsive – Repetitive – Amorous – Personality – that's what I've got, that's what I am.

I am C.R.A.P. and it feels like it sounds.

It's always been a part of me. Teachers at school, friends, really good footballers, cool singers, TV personalities... Kathleen Turner. I liked them a bit too much. It made my insides feel all squishy and my cheeks go red. I'm a blusher – that's crap, I can tell you. Showing the turmoil of your emotional being though a rush of blood to the cheeks – I think I'd be less embarrassed by a permanent erection, although a stiffy might be a distraction during interviews, or on the bus, that sort of thing. To be honest, it would only be a *minor* distraction and only to those with *very* good eyesight.

But I feel it, you know. The fluttering, the elation, the despair of like that goes a bit too far. It turns into another four-letter word altogether – just a little bit. Well, quite a lot actually. You think I'm talking about love, don't you? I am in a way. But it hadn't ever really got that far, not in real life. So, in my experience, what I'm really talking about is 'The Fall'.

Kathleen Turner – *whoa*. Her eyes, her voice, her sass, not to mention her... aesthetic charm. Kathleen, of course, will never know of my undying ardour because we don't mix in the same circles. She has never, to my knowledge, been seen in Lidl's in Brislington. If I saw her there, reaching for the same two-litre bottle of cider as me, I'd be too terrified to speak. She's too perfect and even I know, in my emotional, delusional state, she's more of a vodka and tonic kind of a woman.

If I fell for you, you'd probably never know either – for three reasons.

1. I wouldn't tell you – it saves all the awkwardness on your part and the shrivelling up on mine

2. I wouldn't look at you – not too much, not too close and *not* in your eyes. If you were to look at me back, you'd see what you meant to me and I would combust, spontaneously and fast track my demise into a pile of ashes

3. After a period of inevitable unrequited devotion, I'd fall for someone else – and although I would always, always, carry a candle for you, if not a flaming torch anymore... I'd have moved on

I idolise and swoon from a safe distance. Should we have cause to speak, in some form of transaction or a social interaction, I would hold my eyes open-wide, in a gesture that says I am attentive and focused and slightly adoring – slash – looking quite surprised and a lot like a nutter. I would want to know more, I would want to understand more and I would buy all of your films, books, records, DVDs, pies and other wares to demonstrate – if only to me – the true extent of my feelings.

I would friend you, follow you, comment, like, share and retweet you. I would use a full array of emojis to show you I care @CRAP #fallingforyou – smiley face, winking face, heart.

That is, until Christmas, when I fully expect to fall for the writer of this year's John Lewis ad, or the singer of the song, or the old man on the moon, or penguin or whoever is the central character of this year's story.

Sorry.

But I have a feeling that Christmas might be a bit different this year. Very different.

You see, I've been drinking quite a lot lately – two litre bottles of cider, sometimes one a night. I've been going to Lidl's in Brislington quite a lot lately too, to re-supply and carefully choose the right queue to queue in. So that Kathleen Turner, working on the till, can say the magic words, "That'll be £1.99 please."

It's not Kathleen Turner herself, of course. It's Shelley.

Her voice isn't husky and American, it's bubbly and Bristolian.

Her eyes are beautiful and brown and I have looked at them for a fleeting second and looked away again quickly, so as not to burst into flames – starting with my fiery cheeks and burning down as quickly as a match.

I've not looked at her arse because it's not about

comparisons or relevant, if I'm honest – because of 'The Fall' and because I have fallen.

After a month, we said hello like acquaintances, after two it was like friends. Shelley broke the ice by commenting on my *Game of Thrones* T-shirt. We have that and cider in common. I started to buy more shopping so we could chat over the beep of the bar code scanner.

In the third month, we agreed to re-watch *Game of Thrones* from the start – but in sync, episode by episode. In our stolen, daily chats, we'd allow ourselves 30 seconds of excitement over a dragon, a death or a battle. The best 30 seconds of my day, five days a week. I knew it was serious when I didn't fall for Amelia Clarke... again.

And then, I stopped buying cider altogether. There was a practical dimension to this, I had 47 unopened plastic two-litre bottles in my flat. And there were other reasons too. Shelley counted them, in my flat, when she came round to watch episode four of series three with me. Her favourite. She talked to me afterwards for as long as the programme itself. Just as I thought she was going to go home, she said, "Come on then, episode five and... er... don't s'pose you've got any cider in, have you?"

Did I tell you her eyes were beautiful? Never more so than at that moment and every moment since.

It turns out that Shelley and I have an awful lot in common as well as *Game of Thrones*. She is C.R.A.P. – as C.R.A.P. as I have ever been. All the men on *Strictly*, a barista, Mickey Mouse, Caitlin Moran and Michael Ball. You know it's bad when it's Michael Ball, right?

You might think, now I have confirmed that there're two of us with the condition, I should write to the

General Medical Council to get C.R.A.P. properly registered and to get some appropriate treatment for us both. Well, I'm not.

Our homeopathic remedy of choice is pizza, taken with a drink, of course.

Our therapy sessions are administered via Sky+ and week after week after week, we seem to be getting better.

I have fallen, like I've never fallen before... for Shelley.

And to my amazement, my gratitude and with a lot more floor space now we're finishing off the cider... Shelley has fallen for me.

So, I must apologise if you were looking forward to me shagging your leg – it's just not going to happen.

And it's not going to happen because Shelley and I are a C.R.A.P. couple.

We're so compulsive, repetitive and amorous, we could be in *Game of Thrones* ourselves. I'll leave you with that mental image and hope it doesn't ruin your night.

I'm off home now, to look into Shelley's eyes another 100 times and I do not doubt that I will experience 'The Fall', for each and every one of them.

~

Mark Rutterford's Biography

Mark Rutterford writes and performs his short stories in towns and cities across the South West. Stories with a love interest, a bit of humour, a slice of heartache and, quite often, a prop in hand. If you see him live, it is obvious that the performance element of sharing his work is really important to Mark.

A proud member of Stokes Croft Writers, Mark has written stories featuring badgers, squirrels, aliens and biscuits. Mark is currently eating too many biscuits whilst writing blogs about story telling events he has fallen in love with. If you meet him, please DO NOT feed him – least of all biscuits. In the unlikely event that he does not burst before publication of this anthology, he will be really pleased to be here.

Website: www.markrutterford.com

Twitter: @writingsett

Facebook: www.facebook.com/MarkRutterfordWrites

~

Mark's Competition Judging Comments

Writing, lovely writing. Thank you.

You might think humorous means comic – stories full of gags and the story arc just to get to the next punchline.

To Hull And Back has never been that.

There were some belly-laugh moments for sure, but lots of smartly crafted writing and amazing originality.

It has been a pleasure to read the shortlist – each and every one. But I can't stress enough, just how difficult and, therefore, just how personal the differentiation between stories had to be.

Congratulations to everyone in the anthology – you made for a great read.

POVERTY GAP

Judge's story, by Mike Scott Thomson

Good afternoon, doctor.

Indeed, it hath been a while. I ought to come more often for a dental appointment but, quite frankly, there hath been no need. Thankth to the thterling work your father did on me when I wath a thmall boy, my teeth are thtill in a thplendid condithion.

Well... quite. Up until thith afternoon.

Ought I lie down? Thank you. By all meanth, have a poke around in there.

Aaaaaaaaaar.

Ah-gugugugug.

Yeth, it ith a bit of a meth, ithn't it? Yeth, it duth hurt rather. Thum painkillerth? That would be motht welcome, thank you, thir.

Hmm. Laughing gath? Why not? Thtrap it on and turn it up.

Oooooh, my word. What a delightful thenthathion. While it taikth full effect, I can regale you with my tale. Do ekthcuthe my occathional thtruggle with the odd utteranth while I try to ekthplain.

Due to the fact I am a gentleman with an ethic of fair play, it ith my belief that inthtilling a healthy competitive bulldog thpirit in our nathion'th youth formth the bedrock of a tholid thothiety. No thport can fulfil the brief better than Athothiathian Football, in my humble opinion. For thith reathon, every Thaturday afternoon I pull on my old black rugger top, thling my thilver whithle around my neck and undertake the role of referee, adjudicating between competing academeeth within our ethteemed Five Counteeth League for under theventeenth.

No, good heaventh, never involving Blythe Hall – the Football Athothiathion would never allow it. I am, after all, that ethtablithment'th headmathter. But the teamth involved, while from inthtituthionth of learning not ath high a calibre ath our own, are, on the whole, all-round good eggth.

By Jove, that gath ith doing me the world of good.

Haha. Anyhow. When the new fikthture litht wath dithtributed a few dayth ago, I wath thomewhat contherned to dithcover that in lieu of the unfortunately relegated Thaint Bernard'th Catholic Thchool For Boyth wath a team promoted from League Two, namely, North Grumpton Comprehenthive.

How a team of undithiplined ruffianth had the wherewithal to achieve the lofty height of the County Premier League ith beyond me. Yet fate obliged me to attend the detholate turf of North Grumpton, in order to referee their inaugural top-flight home game againtht the better-bred youngthterth of Barrowford Manor.

I wath not unfamiliar with the area. Backing onto the thchool'th football pitch one will find the 18th fairway of Pettifer'th Golf and Country Club. From here, after many thatithfactory roundth endeavouring to improve my 10 handicap, I have frequently beheld their ill-manicured playing fieldth. A blathted heath indeed, my good thir. Hahaha.

And therefore, for the firtht time in my life, I drove my Jaguar not to the golf club, but rather to the grey, potted tarmac of the Comprehenthive. Ath I pulled up, it wath to my conthternathion I happened to catch thight of two thpethific fellowth amid the cluthter of playerth congregating on the fringeth of the field. Why ought I notith theeth two particularly, you may athk?

The younger of the two, you thee, wath a teenage whipperthnapper by the name of Kevin Crumpkin; the father, a greathy layabout called Keith. Naturally, the prethenth of thothe Neanderthalth would never, in normal thircumthtantheth, trouble me whatthoever; yet I wath familiar with them due to an ekhtraordinary quirk of both fate and fortune within the Crumpkin clan.

Thix numberth; one lottery ticket; one gigantic win. The Crumpkin clan, having mithpent their entire ekhithtenth thponging off the thtate, were thuddenly rewarded for their wanton bone-idleneth to the tune of nearly two million poundth. Thoon afterwardth came an applicathion for young Kevin to attend the hallowed groundth of Blythe Hall; naturally, for that bunch, our fee of nine grand per term had now become mere pin money. Before I knew it, my admithionth department had carelethly welcomed that unbecoming child into our ethtablithment.

Needleth to thay, with hith thickly pallor, cold dead eyth and thatch of perthithtently uncombed hair, he thtood out like a thore thumb. I waited, for one term then two, for hith firtht (and, God willing, final) thignificant indethcrethion, yet none fore came. Even hith ektham markth were above average.

Hahahahahaha. Oh, do ekthcuthe me, doctor. I theem to have forgotten how to thpeak. Where wath I?

Oh yeth. Ath it tranthpired, fate intervened for a thecond time. Clearly the ill-gotten gainth by the Crumpkin family had taught them nary one thcrap of withdom, for by the end of Lent half, young Kevin withdrew. The money, apparently, had run out. Where had it gone? Fatht carth, bad invethtmenth, ekthpenthive holidayth? Who knowth what decadenth made them live beyond their meanth? All that wath apparent ith that the Crumpkinth found themthelvth back in the natural habitat of their old counthil flat, and Kevin made hith leth-than-triumphant return to North Grumpton Comprehenthive: an unholy prodigal thon.

And now there he thtood, ready to play in the thtarting 11 for hith thoccer team. I curthed my mithfortune ath I thtrode onto the pitch to commenth protheedingth.

It wath evident from my firtht whithtle that both teamth were full of pith and vinegar. A crunching tackle from the Barrowford Manor number four on the Grumpton number eight I let go; one doth not want to tarnith a game too early by produthing a yellow card.

Yet I maintain I had no choith when the thentre-half for Grumpton, a burly oik whooth eyebrowth met in the middle of hith forehead, roughly manhandled Mungo Jefferthon-Tompkin by the far corner flag.

Oh, you know Mungo? He'th your brother-in-law'th couthin, you thay? Thmall world it ith indeed good doctor, thmall world. Hahahahahaha.

Anyway, after cauthioning the uncouth lad for unthporting behaviour and thrugging away the howlth of protetht, the remainder of the game, until the very end at leatht, continued without major inthident. Both teamth were toothleth in attack — and the only goal, a fortunate toe-poke on the thtroke of half-time from the wiry Grumpton thtriker, Bruton, I had no choith but to dithallow. He wath, I inthitht, offthide. I told the irate team, who crowded around me thcreaming oath at ear-thplitting volume: two incheth may only be two incheth, but thutch dithtanth ith thtill offthide. No goal.

Now throughout all thith time there wath one player who, thutch wath hith thtraight-and-narrow work ethic on the left flank, could have been invithible. Indeed, Kevin Crumpkin wath to my mind induthtriouth yet oddly quiet. Hith tackelth were perfectly timed and ekthecuted thafely — hith defenthive headerth, robutht and athured. You thee, I give credit where credit ith due. I never wunth found a reathon for booking him.

Until, that ith, the 90th minute. The thcorth were thtuck at nil-nil — neither team had managed to breach the defenth of the other — when it wath my pleathure to award Barrowford Manor a rare but undeniable corner kick. There occurred one thkillfully-taken inthwinging croth into the bokth and, for wunth, North Grumpton failed to clear. Like a thalmon rithing from the othean, there rothe your man, Mungo, and with a fortheful nod of hith head, powered the ball towardth the oppothithion'th net.

Alath, it wath no goal; itth path wath thtopped on the line by the thin, untidy frame of the young defender, Crumpkin. I blew my whithtle. "Handball," I proclaimed, pointing to the faded 12 yard thpot. "Penalty kick."

A gathp arothe from the field, followed by a contemptuouth roar from the oppothithion and their thupporterth. Oh yeth, naturally they protethted, I would thay a little too much. 10 of their playerht thurrounded me in that penalty bokth. "Never a handball," they yelled in unithon. "Look at hith thirt," they cried. "The mud ith on hith chetht, not hith thleeve," and hollow wordth to that effect.

"Thorry," I retorted, affecting an air of thtoithithm – thtoweeethithm – fortitude, ath I reached into my pocket. "Red card for the number three." I produthed the crimthon ticket of doom to Crumpkin, the thingle player not fighting hith own battle, ath he looked down at hith muddy feet, hanging hith head.

From behind me came a tap on my arm. "Oi."

I turned. It wath Keith. The thenior Crumpkin. Thquare chethted and muthcular, with ugly green tattooth covering both bithepth, he wath every inch in body what hiht boy wath not.

"You finally got your moment, didn't you?" he bellowed. "You were waitin' and waitin' to get at my family. And now you've done it. Well, I hope you're bloody happy." And he lifted hith fitht, a meaty knot of thinew and bone, the letterth H, A, T and E tattooed upon hith knuckelth.

I kept calm. "Thir," I thaid, without the lithp of courth, "pleath get off the pitch and let uth finith the game."

He drew hith conthiderable arm back, ready to thtrike me in the mouth. "I'm gonna give you what-for," he growled.

I felt my entrailth twitht and plunge. I have never hit anyone in my life – not thinth corporal punithment wath outlawed, at any rate – and needleth to thay, pugilithm hath never been my cup of tea. I frothe to the thpot, thtaring at the vulgar brute, prepared for that fateful blow.

Behind me came a thmall voith. "Dad, no."

Crumpkin thenior twitched and glanthed over my thoulder; hethitantly, I turned. Kevin wath thtaring at hith animal of a father, bottom lip trembling. "Don't, Dad," he pleaded again. "Not here. It ain't worth it."

Keith Crumpkin'th fitht lowered a little; hith fiery eyth thwitched back to me. "You're right, my boy," thaid he, "Lord Muck here ain't worth it." And he laughed. "Ha," he guffawed. "Not worth a monkey bollock." I would have flinched at thutch uncouth language, but the truth ith, I wath merely relieved I had thumhow ethcaped a beating. "Come on, boy," continued Crumpkin thenior. And both of them, thug father and hith melancholy waif of a thon, trundled off the pitch together, the latter having been red-carded.

I turned back to the athembled playerth. "Now," I thaid, "where were we?"

"Four," came a holler from the far corner of the field.

I turned around, wondering the meaning of thutch a curiouth heckle. Who wath it? Keith Crumpkin? A member of the crowd? I frowned.

"FOUR," came the voith again, equally dithtant but louder. What had that to do with anything? The thcore wath nil-nil. Thoon to be one-nil to Barrowford Manor.

I continued to frown. "Pardon?" I retorted.

And that ith when the golf ball hit me in the mouth and knocked out my two front teeth.

Hahahahahahahahahahahahahahaha...

No, doctor, it ith indeed no laughing matter.

Tho, am I now thuitably thedated for the operathion? I thay, that ith a big needle... I thould lie back and think of England, what? Hahahahahahahahahahahaha... ow, that thmartth... that thmztztztz...

zzzzzzzzzzzzz

*

Urrgggggghhhhhhhh.

Eeeerrrrrgh.

Oh, hello, doctor. All done already? How long was I out for?

Three hours? My word, that must have been quite a mess you had to fix.

Oh, heavens.

Ah-la-la-la-la-la.

Let me look.

Eeeeeeeeee. Aaaaaaaarrrrr.

Oh, my good sir, you've done a wonderful job. A truly excellent job. A splendid, super, sumptuous job.

Down the slippery slide they slid, sitting slightly sideways.

Oh, doctor, it's better than I could have hoped.

Now, how much do I owe you?

I *beg* your pardon?

How much?

~

Mike Scott Thomson's Biography

Mike Scott Thomson has been writing fictions of various lengths since 2011. Over the year's they've been either shrinking into flash fictions, or are threatening to expand into novellas or, fate willing, a novel. Publication credits include stories published in three Fiction Desk anthologies, the literary magazines *Litro, Prole,* and *Storgy,* and competition placings from Momaya Press, InkTears, *Writers' Forum,* and Chris Fielden's own inaugural To Hull And Back competition.

In 2016, he accidentally challenged the literary community to use as many adverbs as they could possibly manage, in stories of fewer than 100 words. Four successful charity anthologies later, he's still not entirely sure what happened, but he's very glad it did.

Website: www.mikescottthomson.com

Twitter: @michaelsthomson

~

Mike's Competition Judging Comments

I've assisted with the judging of the competition on a few occasions now, and it doesn't get any easier. What a terrific selection of short stories. Just like the number of entries, the standard seems to rise year on year. How on Earth does anyone filter out the best of the lot?

As ever, it was helpful for me to use the judging criteria as suggested by Chris – for example, marks for openings and endings, strength of prose, humour – but even that ultimately comes down to subjectivity and personal taste. Every judge would have reported back with very different lists. It couldn't be any other way.

Like on previous occasions, helping with this competition has again been a valuable learning process for me; certainly a reminder of where my own writing can be improved, and that I should probably step up my game. So to all on the shortlist: thank you for that. And for the ultimate winner, who at the time of writing is as yet unannounced — hearty congratulations. Enjoy your stint on The Hog.

THE HERO

Judge's story, by John Holland

Since I started growing my hair, the neighbours – the men – have stopped speaking to me. Although their wives still do.

"Your hair's growing, John."

"Can't stop it, Mrs Wilkinson."

It's teatime. I'm striding home from school, past the rows of semis in the next street to mine, when I see Mr Wilkinson, in his frameless spectacles, walking towards me. It's too late to cross the road. I know he won't speak. And I won't either. But as he approaches he lets out a broad smile, and says, "Your dad did well, didn't he?"

"Yeah," I say. And then we have passed.

I have no idea what he means.

By the time I push open the backdoor of our semi, painted a tawdry yellow, it has left my mind.

"What would you like for tea?" It's my mum. Dad doesn't get home for ages so we eat without him.

"Steak and kidney pie, chips and peas," I say.

"Hard luck," she says.

It's not just the luck that's hard. The crusts on these luncheon meat and salad cream sandwiches taste like they have been rusting away behind the shed with the rest of Dad's collection of 'useful' metal parts.

"Chef quit?" I ask, joking.

"Sacked," she says.

There are three places set at the dining table. I sit at one end where I can swivel to watch teatime TV. Opposite me is my dad's place, awaiting his arrival in an hour or two. Mum sits between us. Symbolically probably. With her back to the TV. Opposite her is the hatch to the kitchen that my dad made for the passing of plates of food. Plates of food so hot that they melt the skin on your fingers.

"Why don't you sit in dad's place, so you can watch *Zoo Time*, Mum?"

"*Zoo Time*, Schmoo Time," she says, pretending to be Jewish.

Desmond Morris, with a comb-over that risks him being flagellated to death on a windy day, is cuddling a jaguar cub.

"Lovely," says Mum, without turning. "Although many people confuse jaguars with leopards. The jaguar is a South American mammal, the leopard is African. They don't really have spots. More sort of circular rosettes. Jaguars tend to have larger rosettes with spots in the middle; the leopard has plain rosettes with no central spot."

It's impressive. Within seconds, Desmond says the same thing about jaguars and leopards.

"You the script writer?" I ask

"Your hair's getting long," she says.

"You will tell me when it actually is long, won't you?" I say, tossing my head so that my hair flies from one side and meets me on the other.

"Probably not," she replies. "You'd never hear me through all that hair."

She remembers. "Isn't it great about Dad?"

But I'm heading for the front room and my homework.

The front room is the better, less-used room – grey sofa, two grey arm chairs, my dad's tropical aquarium, the Dansette record player on the floor and the golden plastic hostess trolley, which is thought to be posher than the wooden one in the dining room. But no TV or table. I use the seat of an armchair to kneel and write. The front room is also where I entertain my girlfriend, Janet. She is due at 7.30. A switchboard operator at the Gas Board, she is unencumbered by homework. I have about an hour and a half for A level geography.

The fishing industry in the Adriatic Sea makes me wish I'd taken history. But I enjoy the names of the principally caught species – common dentex, red scorpion fish, monkfish, John Dory, spiny dogfish, Norway lobster (surely a long way from home), mullet and red mullet. I wonder what colour the mullet are that are not red. And whether the two species clash, at least aesthetically. Mum would know.

I'm entering Trieste as I hear Dad arrive home and go straight to the dining room for his tea.

I finish the homework without feeling the need to get the definitive word on the colour of the non-red mullet. And gratify myself with the double LP *Bitches Brew* by Miles Davis that I'd bought in town on Saturday. I hold it by its pristine edges. Slide one of the black discs, with its orange labelled centre, from its white inner sleeve and place it on the Dansette, dropping the stylus arm carefully onto the spinning vinyl. The music crackles into life. I gaze at the distorted yellow orange figures on the album cover while extraordinary sounds fill the room.

I am in a voodoo opium den in Harlem.

I see the handle of the door turn. I imagine a Chinese dealer with a coloured silk hat and a braided ponytail. Mum's head appears. It listens for a split second.

"Is that Herbie Hancock on an electric piano — something of a departure for him, isn't it?" she asks.

I check the sleeve. And nod in resignation.

"You've been looking at the cover, haven't you?" I say.

She shrugs the one shoulder I can see in the half-opened doorway and recites from memory the band's entire 14-strong line up from Bennie Maupin on bass clarinet to Jack DeJohnette on drums — right channel, and Lenny White, drums — left channel. Although with only one speaker channel on the tinny Dansette that's academic.

"You're not normal," I tell her.

"Your dad's here, you know, if you want to ask him," she says and disappears.

But, as I stand I hear the doorbell.

Janet, in all her darkness, has arrived. I look at my watch.

"Just four and a half minutes late," I tell her.

If a face can shrug hers does. I get a lukewarm half-kiss. She doesn't have her dog – a boxer – with her. I'm relieved. It salivates when we are at our loving. Glutinous strings hanging from its mouth to its chest and even the floor. And that sad face it pulls.

The upside to the dog is that I can blame him when Mum complains about suspicious wet marks on the carpet or rug.

Janet and I have been going out for nearly two years, and have a routine. She comes round to mine three times a week and I go round to hers less often – because it's not so convenient for me. Saturday we go to the pub, or the pictures, or a party.

I help her off with her sheepskin coat, and open the door to the front room, from which emerges the sound of Miles and those 14 named individuals blazing a riotous storm.

"What the bloody hell's this?" she says.

I tell her. She says nothing. As usual, I sit in the grey armchair next to the fish tank. She sits on my knee. We kiss properly, and I announce that tonight I will be removing her bra single-handed.

"Not getting one of your mates to help?" she says, throwing back her black hair.

"No, I mean I won't use two hands. You know, I'll be smooth and a bit sharp, like James Bond or someone." I hold my face at an angle I think is smooth and a bit sharp.

"We'll see," she says. "You know your hair's getting really long."

"I had no idea," I say, pulling up the back of her red

woollen jumper and weighing up the opposition. It's an old adversary – the white bra with lace between the cup and the straps. It has three pairs of hooks.

"My mate Geoff says Diane has one that unloads at the front," I tell her.

"Like one of those new washing machines," she says. "I bet he doesn't play her shit music like this."

It's not the best moment for romance. But there follows a lengthy period, with her jumper pulled up, in which my right hand pinches and squeezes the back of the bra with a combination of finger-numbing tension and bloody-minded determination, for which even Wayne Shorter's exquisite tenor sax solo is not an appropriate soundtrack. Finally, I admit defeat.

"I'll get you a mannequin for your birthday. You can practice in the comfort of your own room," she tells me.

"And a supply of bras," I add.

My dad never enters the front room when we are there, but mum normally comes in about 10.00, always turning the door handle artificially slowly whilst rattling it, so it makes as much noise as possible.

She did catch us on one occasion, but told us not to worry because she was young once. We doubted that.

10.30 is the time I walk Janet home.

And, at exactly 10.30, I shout to my parents, "See you later," before closing the back door and walking Janet almost silently in the chilly darkness through our estate, along the main road, until the sickly odour of the Lanolin factory is obliterated by the salt and vinegar smell of Pauline's Fish Bar. Then between the high rise flats to her parents' terraced house. In the lamp-lit alleyway, I kiss her goodnight. Watch her walk up the stone steps to her parents' back door. As she turns to call her final goodnight, she shouts out, "Great about your dad." Then closes the door before I can ask her. She knows about Dad. Perhaps the whole town does.

When I arrive home my parents are in bed.

As usual, Dad leaves early for work the next morning, so I don't see him, but the first thing I do when I get up is to ask Mum what he did.

"You mean you don't know?" she shouts, laughing.

"No, I do not," I say.

"W-e-l-l," she says, rolling her tongue around her mouth to mark the fact a story is to follow. "Yesterday lunchtime, when you were at school, Dad was walking home from work when there, in the avenue, was this huge bull. I think it was a Holstein Fresian. They're sort of black red in colour with white patches, and originate from cattle bred on the island of Batavia between the Rhine, the Maas and the Waal."

"Yes, yes, yes. What happened?"

"It was in a truck bound for the abattoir," she says. "But escaped. Your dad grabbed it by the nose ring, and calmly walked it back to the truck."

"What?" I yell. "Surely that's not true. How did it get out of the wagon? Why was a wagon, carrying a bull bound for slaughter, driving through the estate? Why didn't it gore Dad, or run away from him? How did they get it back in the vehicle? I have these and other questions," I say.

"Your dad used to work in an abattoir before the war, you know. Bulls are a speciality of his."

"That's a sentence I never thought I'd hear."

"That's your dad, isn't it?" says Mum.

The phone rings. Unusual for 8am. It's Janet.

"Hello, my love. This isn't in today's programme," I say.

"Look," she says, "I'm dumping you."

"Why beat about the bush?" I say.

"I want to go out with other boys. With men," she says pointedly.

"Are you saying that I'm not manly enough?"

"I would never say that, but yes, you're not manly enough. You'd never tame a wild bull like your dad did, would you? Not with that hair."

"I might."

"You're an idiot," she says.

"You used to think I was funny," I say.

The phone goes dead.

My mind is fireworks. I wonder what Miles Davis would have done. His father was a dentist and never went near animals. Maybe if I'd been born black this would never have happened. Or played the trumpet. Or owned one I couldn't play. Kept it on top of the bookcase.

I go into the kitchen to tell Mum. With black biro and pad of paper, she's noting down all the players from Yorkshire football clubs who played international football for the home nations. It's quite a short list.

"Did Denis Law play for Scotland as a teenager with Huddersfield Town?" she asks.

"Can't help you, Mum," I say, and break the news about Janet. She winds her arms around me, folds me in her Luncheon Meat, Leopard Spots, Lenny White Drumming, Denis Law love. And, as she holds me, she has to blow my hair away from her mouth.

"Do you think you might get it cut now?" she asks.

"Probably," I say.

~

John Holland's Biography

John Holland is a short fiction author from Stroud in Gloucestershire. He started writing stories when he was 59.

As well as winning first prize in the 2018 To Hull And Back Short Story Competition, John has also won first prize in competitions run by the Dorset Fiction Award, InkTears, Momaya Press and the Worcestershire LitFest. His stories have been short/long listed in a further 40 competitions.

John's work has been extensively published in print and online, and he isn't far from having his hundredth piece published. As well as the *To Hull And Back Anthology*, his work is in the *Bath Short Story Award Anthology, The Best Stories in a Decade* (Momaya Press), *The National Flash Fiction Day Anthology* and elsewhere, and online at Reflex Fiction, The Cabinet of Heed, The Molotov Cocktail, EllipsisZine, NFFD and others.

He likes to read to audiences, particularly if they're drunk, and has done so in many places including London, Birmingham, Bath, Bristol, Stroud and the Cheltenham Literature Festival.

John is the organiser of the twice-yearly event, Stroud Short Stories, described by the Cheltenham LitFest as 'possibly the best short story event in the South West'.

'The Hero' was first published by the online literary journal *The Cabinet of Heed,* Issue 16, January 2019.

Website: www.johnhollandwrites.com

SSS website: www.stroudshortstories.blogspot.com

~

John's Competition Judging Comments

By dint of having won this wonderful short story competition in 2018, I was asked by Chris Fielden to be one of the judges for To Hull And Back 2019. I consider it a huge honour.

Being the organiser and twice yearly co-judge of the Stroud Short Stories (SSS) events, and the former judge of The Evesham Festival of Words Short Story Competition, I had some insight into the sheer variety of styles, tones and subject matter which emerge from the strangely brilliant minds of writers.

However, for SSS we just choose 10 stories to be read by their authors at our events. There's no winner. For Chris, the task was to put the uniformly entertaining, but very varied, stories in the 20-strong shortlist in order from 1 to 20 – *what a challenge.*

I enjoyed all the stories and, as it was, there were three stories that blew my mind, and for which I would gladly have traded my wife and my children to read. But which of the three was best?

And then there were the others, which I would happily have traded my house and my collection of Wolverhampton Wanderers memorabilia just to be near. But which was fourth and which was sixteenth?

As I write, I don't know the final winners after all the judges votes have been correlated. I hope it's the same as the ones I chose. But it won't be, will it? Judging is a highly subjective exercise and don't let anyone tell you otherwise.

Congratulations to everyone who made the shortlist and the anthology. I love you.

THE KEITH OF DEATH

Judge's story, by Christopher Fielden

I'm in Debenhams' menswear department, trying to work out if the rhino is real. I've been self-medicating for my headaches and, I admit, sometimes I can be a little overzealous with my dosage. The tablets look like Skittles and, well, I like Skittles.

The rhino is grazing on socks, snarling, revealing more pointed teeth than you'd expect to find in a herbivore. Its skin is white and its body shimmers like a glacier in the sun. Black tendrils of electricity fizz around its horn.

I've almost convinced myself that the rhinoceros is a hallucination, when I feel a hand on my arm.

"Is that a rhino?"

I glance to my left and see a dude clasping a selection pack of boxer shorts so tightly that his knuckles look like alabaster.

"You can see it too?" I ask.

He nods.

We both gawp at the rhino, transfixed.

I'm just beginning to think the rhino is real when a thought occurs to me. Maybe the dude is a figment of my imagination too? I turn to study him.

He's middle-aged and rotund, built like a beach ball. Beads of sweat glisten above his googly eyes and his nasal hair is mesmerising; every time he breathes out it dances like seaweed in a neap tide. Hmm. He looks real. How can I be sure? I punch him in the arm, harder than I intended. He stumbles sideways.

"What the...?" He regains his balance and punches me in the face. It hurts. He's definitely real.

As I dab at the blood trickling from my nose, I see the rhino rise onto its hind legs and walk towards us. With each step it takes, threads of ice crawl from its feet, clawing at the floor tiles like they're alive.

The rhino growls. My balls tingle. This feels very real and very amiss. Still, me and Punchy both stand there, hypnotised. Are you supposed to be aggressive and try to look big when facing a rhino, like you would a bear? Or cower? Or run? Are there different rules when the rhino can walk on its hind legs? I don't remember David Attenborough dealing with any of this.

The rhino stops its advance and looks through us with dead eyes. "Keith," it says, nodding at me. "Desmond." It nods at Punchy. "Two at once. What fun." Its voice is guttural.

"Wha'?" I manage, after the silence becomes uncomfortable.

"I'm the Rhino of Death," says the Rhino of Death. "You're both dead."

"Wha'?" says Desmond.

"Take as long as you need," says the rhino.

It turns out me and Punchy Des need a substantial amount of time.

I look around. I see a body lying in the bra aisle. Wait. Not a body. My body (I came in here for socks, but the menswear department is right next to the womenswear department and, well, I like bras). It's not just my body; it's my body with a stiletto sticking out of its skull. Punchy Des's body is in the same state next to a rack of boxer shorts.

"What happened to us?" I ask.

"You're the first victims of the Stiletto Psycho," says the Rhino of Death, "a killer destined to be more famous than Jack the Ripper. Your murders will be dramatized by the BBC for centuries."

"Lucky us."

"Quite."

"So, is this heaven?" asks Punchy Des.

"Debenhams' menswear department?" The rhino chuckles, causing icy flakes to rise from its nostrils. They twinkle eerily in the artificial lighting. "No."

"So, what happens now?" I ask.

"We must race." There's an unpleasant glint in the rhino's black eyes. It's toying with us. "If you win, eternity will be yours."

"And if we lose?"

A white, forked tongue flickers between the rhino's teeth. "You will be mine."

I have the distinct feeling that wouldn't be good. "Where do we race to?"

"Well, 'race' is probably the wrong word," says the Rhino of Death. "'Hunt' might be more appropriate."

"Hunt?"

"It works like this. You run. I'll count to ten. Then I'll try to find you."

Debenhams usually feels so calm and relaxing. So normal. Today, it feels demonic. The air is freezing and my core feels cold, like my soul is being stalked. I'm not a crier, but I feel a tear run down my cheek. The thought of playing a child's game with this creature seems terrifying.

I look at Punchy Des. He's in a worse state than me. In addition to tears, snot hangs from his nose, dampening his nasal-mane's hypnotic dance. "This isn't what's supposed to happen when you die," he says.

"What is?" The rhino's smile is devoid of empathy.

"I dunno," he says. "But not this."

"If you think life was unfair, wait until you better understand death." The rhino takes a step towards us. The cold radiating from the creature is so intense it hurts. "I'd start running if I were you." The rhino turns his back on us. "Ten."

Punchy Des gawps at me.

"Nine."

Des turns and runs, knocking over a mannequin dressed in revealing red underwear, before getting on the up escalator. Up? I'd have chosen down. Maybe that's what the rhino expects. Go, Punchy Des, be luckier in death than you were in life.

"Eight."

I'm not a big fan of running. I lack the coordination to do anything gracefully, especially at speed.

"Seven."

And I'm pretty sure running is pointless. There was a glint in the rhino's eyes that suggested the hunt was a formality, the game had already been won.

"Six."

I look around for a weapon. There's lots of men's clothing. None of it could really be used effectively to attack anyone. Or in defence. I could go and find a stiletto. Even that wouldn't be much use against an undead rhinoceros.

"Five."

I could hide. But where? I have a feeling hiding would be even less use than running. Standing there with its back to me, the rhino looks like a smoke machine that's malfunctioned. Icy fog billows from its shoulders.

"Four."

I reach into my pocket, pull out my fags and light one. Well, I wasn't expecting that to work. Apparently being dead sucks in every way imaginable, but you can still smoke.

"Three."

I take a long drag and study the perfectly formed cylinder of smoky wonderment held between my thumb and forefinger. I purse my lips and blow smoke at my fag. Ash crumbles from the end, revealing a glowing tip.

"Two."

I look at the rhino. The cold rhino. And then back at my cigarette. My hot cigarette.

"One."

I take one more drag. I'm not the hunted. I'm the

hunter. And my weapon is a cigarette. A cigarette... A small tube of leaves, smouldering at one end. Hmm. I feel my confidence wane. I probably should've run.

"Ready or not, here I come."

The Rhino of Death spins around. As it sees me standing there, holding my fag like a dagger, the rhino goes from looking all deranged and psycho, like Jack Nicholson busting through that door in *The Shining*, to shocked by something completely unexpected, like the crew of the Nostromo when that baby alien explodes out of John Hurt's chest.

The rhino falters. I stab at it with my cigarette. I'm lucky; the ciggy strikes, the tip sizzling on the base of the rhino's horn.

Its mouth opens. It's like a shark's. There are thousands of teeth in there, all serrated and gleaming. I think the rhino is going to bite my head off when a high-pitched noise emits from the hole my cigarette left in its horn. I think my ears might explode, but then the rhino explodes instead, into an icy mist. Its horn is all that remains intact. It thuds on the floor.

My cigarette has gone soggy. I discard it and light another. I'm not used to winning, especially that easily. I'm surprised to find I gain no pleasure from it.

I wonder if all of this is just the meds. I've always had a vivid imagination. It tends to get out of control when I'm stimulated. By anything.

I reach into the lingering mist and touch the rhino's horn. It's unbelievably cold. My fingers turn white, like snow. The mist clears and cruel laughter echoes in my head. Shit.

"Is it dead?"

I look around and see Punchy Des. He flinches as he sees me. "Oh, man." He turns and runs.

I feel empty. Not instantly. It's as if my soul is dissolving. I look at the rhino's horn. It's gone. I put a hand to my forehead. I feel an icy protrusion.

As the last of my humanity seeps away, I just have time to realise I didn't win. The rhino caught me.

I sniff the air and taste the aroma of Punchy Des, sweet with fear.

It's time to hunt.

~

Christopher Fielden's Biography

Chris has recently signed a publishing deal with Victorina Press. His collection of short stories, *Book of the Bloodless Volume 1: Alternative Afterlives*, is being released later this year. 'The Keith of Death' is one of those stories. The book has been awarded the title of "Award-Winning Finalist in the 'Fiction: Short Story' category of the 2019 International Book Awards".

Chris's head is now so swollen, he can't move and resides in the Big Head's Wing, a secure unit of the I Can't Quite Believe It, I Need A Lie Down Institute for authors who have lost all sense of the difference between third, second and first person narrative, especially when writing their own biographies.

You notice the last strange sentence and wonder if Chris has lost his mind. After much deliberation, you decide he has. You are correct.

I've been running this celebration of humorous literary masterpieces for six years. I'm astounded, and immensely pleased, that To Hull And Back has grown every time it's been run. Every year, entry numbers go up, anthology sales go up, the prize pot goes up... You get the gist, things go up.

When all this started, I thought the insane top prize might not have a very wide appeal. I'm immensely pleased to have been proved wrong. Long live humour. Long live craziness. Long live laughter. I think we need it at the moment. More than ever.

www.christopherfielden.com/about/

~

Chris's Competition Judging Comments

This year, I received a record number of competition entries, yet again. The history of entry numbers looks like this:

- 2019: 582 (+126)
- 2018: 456 (+97)
- 2017: 359 (+75)
- 2016: 284 (+68)
- 2015: 216 (+122)
- 2014: 94

The early bird fee helped again this year, working in similar fashion to last year. At the end of April 2019, I'd received 212 entries, compared to 208 entries in 2018. Pretty much the same.

The flow of submissions from May through to July was steady, so I managed to stay on top of the reading until mid-July. I'd also cleared the decks of all other projects, which gave me more time to read. Still, there was a big influx of entries as the closing date approached. 312 in the final month, 162 in the final week, 56 on the final day. Last year, it was 187 in the final month, 110 in the final week, 38 on the final day.

Writers do love working right up until a deadline, don't they? Yes. Yes they do...

I know I say this every year, but I'm NOT complaining about the amount of entries I receive – it's fantastic that so many people enter and support the competition. I'm extremely grateful and hope the number of entries continues to grow in the future. I simply share these stats because I find them interesting and it helps me find better ways of running To Hull And Back.

This year, I went to the Llŷn Peninsula in North West Wales to undertake the reading and judging.

I visited my friends, Alison, Jim and Jackson, in Northwich en route. I also went to Bingley, near Leeds, to visit my old work colleague, Dave, and meet his new wife to be, Emily (WHOOP, congrats guys – awesome news).

Then I headed to Wales and camped on the Western tip of the Llŷn Peninsula. I found a lovely spot, parked up and read lots.

On the way home, I visited one of my favourite places – Llŷn Brianne in the Cambrian Mountains in Wales – to make those final tough decisions.

The quality of the stories entered this year was awe-inspiring. There were so many fresh ideas I hadn't seen before. Stories that are imaginative and original resonate with me. I find reading them inspiring.

Due to the ever increasing workload that To Hull And Back generates, I've made the difficult decision to start running the competition biennially in the future. For the past six years, the competition has been open 24/7. I'm only human; I need a break. So the next competition will run in 2021 (opening for entries on 1st August 2020, closing 31st July 2021).

This is to spread the workload and make it manageable. It also means I can look into some admin changes for future competitions. Here are the changes I've decided on, and the ones I'm considering:

- Prize pot increased from £2,750 to £3,250:
  - First: £1,200 (up from £1,000)
  - Second: £600 (up from £500)
  - Third: £300 (up from £250)
  - 3 x Highly Commended: £150 (up from £100)
  - 14 x Shortlisted: £50
  - If we see more growth next time the competition runs, I'll concentrate on increasing the 14 shortlist prizes
- Increased entry fees, to help cover the bigger prize pot and maintain growth:
  - Early-bird entry fee – if you enter the competition before 30th April, you will pay £13 for one story, £21 for two stories, £26 for three stories
  - If you enter between 1st May and 31st July, you will pay £15 for one story, £24 for two stories, £30 for three stories
- Investigate using Submittable to manage and automate the entry process:
  - This would cost money and thus increase the running costs of the competition, but it'll take out a lot of admin and (hopefully) mean fewer rules that are easier to follow
- Look into working with other readers to help manage the judging process and decide the shortlist:

- o This would also be likely to cost money, but it's getting to the stage where selecting the shortlist is too much work for one person
- o Having more readers would also mean a wider variety of styles and genres might start being selected for the shortlist, as this judging malarkey is highly subjective – it might help freshen things up a bit
- Keep trying to get some sponsorship, to help the competition grow

That's it for now, but having a year off will allow me some time to think and consider other ways of improving To Hull And Back in the future.

I hope I'm not putting people off by increasing the entry fee again. It simply allows more growth and makes the risk a little safer for me – if the competition makes a loss, which it has done in the past, I have to cover it. As the prize pot increases, so does the risk of extreme skintness. Putting the entry fee up just makes things a little bit safer for me.

This year, the competition is highly likely to make a profit (as always, it depends on anthology sales), which is why I'm able to consider using Submittable in the future. The 2019 prizes are first £1,000, second £500, third £250, 3 x runner-up prizes of £100 and 14 x shortlist prizes of £50 – total is £2,750.

Other costs include PayPal charges, video production costs, admin costs, website maintenance costs, costs of publishing the anthology, advertising costs, the costs of putting on a book launch and, of course, the epic journey to Hull and back. I also offered a small payment to the artist of the anthology cover for the first time this year. I plan to keep doing that in future.

This year's cover was designed by David Whitlam. Here's the sneaky draft-preview, which was used in a 'your head could be here' style ad on social media.

All the judges and everyone else involved with the competition continue to give their time for free, which I appreciate greatly.

As I've said before, the long-term aim is to provide a five figure top prize to help the competition become more widely known and give humorous short stories a respected publishing platform to be celebrated from. Maybe one day...

Entries this year came from an increasing number of locations around the planet. They include: Australia, Austria, Belgium, Brazil, Canada, China, Croatia, Cyprus, Dominican Republic, England, Finland, France, Germany, Holland, Hong Kong, India, Ireland, Israel, Italy, Japan, Kenya, Mexico, New Zealand, Northern Ireland, Scotland, South Africa, Spain, Sweden, Switzerland, Thailand, Trinidad and Tobago, USA and Wales.

This year, for the first time, I've kept track of different points of view used to tell the stories. Hey, it's interesting if you're a writing geek, and I am one. Here are the figures:

- Stories written in the first person (I did, I said): 47.5%
- Stories written in the second person (you did, you said): 1%
- Stories written in the third person (he did, she said): 50%
- Other (stories that were presented as a script, or an article, or meeting minutes, or used both 1st and 3rd person etc.): 1.5%

In 2018, 37 entries didn't obey the rules (7% of the 456 entries). In 2019, that figure increased to 59 (just over 10% of 582 entries). That's a small increase, so pretty good. Unfortunately, I still had to disqualify 12 stories, but that's fewer than last year (16). Most of the disqualifications were either over the word count limit, or failed to obey any of the rules.

If you weren't longlisted or shortlisted this year, please don't be disheartened. Each year, there are more entries but the same number of places on the short and longlist. I don't reject stories because I don't like them. I simply select the stories that are best suited to this competition.

That's it. Year six is complete. I've read hundreds of stories. I've laughed a lot. I've been inspired, surprised and delighted by some brilliant writing. Thank you to everyone who has entered. This simply would not be possible without each and every one of you.

Cheers me dears, Chris.

THE WORLD IN A FISHBOWL

Judge's story, by Christie Cluett

Janet was looking for the exact colour of ornament to go with the new curtains, bottle green. *Maybe a bottle?* she thought, as she perused the stalls of Geoff and Linda's garage sale. She picked up knickknacks, trinkets, baubles and trifles, trying to work out what visitors would think of each one. She eyed her husband, Martin, as he bartered a little too enthusiastically with Linda over a record player that definitely wasn't coming into her house.

Janet turned the teal figurine in her hands, wondering if it was heavy enough to accidentally cleave Martin's skull in, or if it was just light enough to stop him from laughing in that way. She measured the weight in her hand and then put it back down on the table.

"Darling," Janet said, taking hold of Martin's elbow with her fingernails digging in. He flinched slightly but didn't let his smile slip more than a millimetre. "Seen anything?" She didn't wait for an answer, smiling at Linda. "I love all your things, Linda. Such lovely things. I can't imagine why you're getting rid of them..."

"I know, Janet," Linda said, laughing slightly wildly.

Janet laughed too, not entirely sure what they were laughing at but not wanting to ask in case it was obvious. Soon, Martin joined in and the three of them were laughing at nothing as Geoff finished taking 20p for a Dan Brown hardback. Geoff then nodded and laughed along with them, at God knows what.

"Seen anything, Martin?" Geoff called.

Martin smiled, nodded and laughed.

"I know, Geoff," Martin said. "I know."

Janet laughed while she nodded and Linda joined in, and then the four of them continued to laugh as they tried not to look at each other.

As Janet chuckled to a slow halt, she was met with the beginnings of a silence that loomed towards her. She could see it threatening Martin as he turned his slightly desperate gaze towards her. Janet blinked and looked around her, grabbing the first object she saw, as the laughing stopped.

"Oh, how lovely. This is lovely. Isn't it, Martin?" she

said, at the obviously non-green thing in her hands.

"It certainly is," Martin agreed.

"Oh, yes. It really is," Linda said, taking the clear round fishbowl from Janet's hands as Geoff nodded and smiled his agreement as he backed slowly towards the garage.

"Two pounds to you, Janet," Linda said, as Janet put a hand into her pocket and thrust the bowl into Martin's hands.

"Oh, I'm so pleased we found just the thing. Lovely," Janet said.

"Lovely," they all said in unison as they backed away from each other with wide smiles.

*

Martin put the fishbowl on the side table with a clunk. "Well... That was nice."

Janet sighed as she listened to Martin click on the kettle, humming to himself loudly, a half-tune that she'd been listening to for 22 years. She picked up the bowl, turning it in her hands, measuring the weight and wondered if it would split his scalp or was just light enough to stop him humming for a little while.

She put it back on the table, switching it from the left to the right. As she pushed it back to the centre, she leaned in to flick out a couple of grains of sand left in the bottom, before she went upstairs to lie down under a cold flannel.

*

The next morning, Janet was waiting for the kettle to boil, watching Martin standing in the garden looking over the fence at nothing, as was his habit. She looked at the new fishbowl, wondering where Janet had kept it in her house, and noticed a small patch of sand in the bottom of the bowl. She leaned closer. It hadn't been there yesterday, an obvious increase on the couple of grains that she'd cleared out. She picked it up and emptied it into the sink, before turning her attention to the boiling kettle.

After lunch, after slowly wiping the counter, Janet picked up the bowl and found an inch of sand completely covering the bottom. She opened the back door to shout for Martin, who turned with a faraway look in his eyes.

"Look," she said, thrusting the bowl towards his face. "There's sand in it."

Martin nodded and shrugged as he took it from her and went towards the sink.

"No," she said. "I already tried that."

"Is the tea ready?" he said, but Janet wasn't listening. She was staring at the sand, trying to see if it was getting any bigger.

*

From that day onwards, the fishbowl didn't disappoint Janet's curiosity. The next day, the island of sand had shrunk slightly, but by the evening a ring of water had formed around the outside. Next, a tiny palm tree sprung up in the middle of the island, and then another, finally joined together by a hammock strung between them. Janet peered inside the bowl for hours, as the days passed in heavy silence. Martin only nodded and smiled vaguely until the day they came downstairs and there was a perfectly formed, small, deluxe beach house resting on the island.

"Oh," Martin said, inspecting the overlapping white tiles of the roof and the painted boards of the outside walls. "That guttering needs seeing to."

As they watched, the sand indented slightly along the curve of the shore, and the water began lapping gently until it turned into tiny cresting waves. A seagull popped into existence in the middle of the bowl and went swooping over the whole scene.

A speck of blue became discernible, sweeping around the edge of the bowl. It zoomed past them, getting bigger and bigger, and raced down toward the edge of the sand, finally recognisable as a small car, a convertible. Its wheels gripped the sand as it took off at quite a rate across the sand towards the house.

As it careered along the makeshift road, Janet could see a striped umbrella angled out of the back seat and she caught the high-pitch of a woman's laughter as it was spun up by the wind. She leaned closer and could see a man wearing sunglasses in the front seat, with one hand on the wheel, his arm across the back of the seat behind the blonde girl next to him.

Martin and Janet watched as the tiny car screeched to a halt and the figures leapt out. The girl was wearing figure-hugging red capris and a white shirt tied at the front, revealing a flat, tanned stomach. It reminded Janet of what she used to wear in her younger, firmer days.

The small man in the bowl ran a palm back through his hair, smoothing it down, and smiled off into the distance. Janet noticed Martin absently touch the bald spot at the back of his head, as the man turned with a grin and hauled the woman over his shoulder, running inside to the sound of her delighted giggles.

*

Over the following weeks, the activity in the fishbowl fascinated Janet. She pulled a chair from the dining room as soon as she got home from work, watching the tiny good-looking pair as they sunbathed, as they went for walks hand in hand, as they played volleyball on the sand. She ate her dinner from a plate that she hardly noticed Martin set beside her, sitting with a forkful of mashed potato poised in mid-air until it was cold with a crust.

"We should go on a beach holiday, don't you think, Martin? Martin?"

Martin was waiting for the kettle to boil, staring out of the window at something far in the distance, humming to himself. Janet watched the man in the bowl haul a record player outside. Music Janet remembered from her youth blared out and she wondered if Linda and Geoff danced to their old records.

"Maybe we should learn to dance," she said to Martin's back. She watched the figures sadly as their tiny waists twisted round each other in the sand, not noticing that Martin had stopped humming.

"We should start having sex in the daytime, Martin. Don't you think, Martin?"

Janet jumped suddenly as Martin's fist pounded into the kitchen counter, apparently a final straw.

"No," he said, with his head down. "No, Janet. Enough. I don't want to go on a beach holiday. I don't want to start eating fresh mango. I certainly don't want to learn to surf, and there's absolutely no way that we can have sex standing up. You know I have problems with my knees."

Janet looked up at him, as the tiny couple retreated into the beach house, closing the door quietly behind them.

"I don't want the life of that man in the fishbowl, and neither should you. You know, he's very different when you're not here. That's not the only girl he's brought out to that island, wilfully ignoring the highway code as he endangers everyone's life in that convertible. There are no seatbelts, Janet. No seatbelts. The last time you went to the shop, he turned up with a couple of ladies in hardly any clothing and drawn on eyebrows, and I'm pretty sure they were mother and daughter."

The windows of the beach house snapped shut as shouting from inside rustled the curtains. Janet looked from the bowl to Martin and sighed.

"Mother and daughter, Janet. You want me to be like him, all sunglasses and filling out his trousers?"

Janet raised her eyebrows, about to let out a squeak of, "Well…" before Martin continued, his voice loud and slightly too high.

"You want me to fuck your mother, Janet? Do you? Because I will if that's what you want."

The door to the beach house was ripped open and the woman in her beach shorts and crop top came storming out with a suitcase. She took off across the sand, the heavy case bumping against her legs as the little man in the bowl watched her go, smoking a cigarette with a smirk on his face.

Martin's voice was lower. "I will, if that's what you want, Janet, because I love you."

"Oh, Martin," Janet said, looking away from the bowl. She patted his cheek as she passed on the way to the kitchen. "No. Thanks, but no. I doubt she'd be into it anyway. Her and Dennis from across the way are experimenting with BDSM."

Martin nodded, looking relieved.

*

Martin watched Janet pick up the kettle and sat down to wait for the tea. He didn't hear the click, though, and was surprised when Janet came marching back with the full kettle. She had a determined look in her eye that he'd seen during Christmas supermarket trips. She slowly poured the water into the fishbowl.

They both watched the gradual rise of the tide mark as the edges of the island began to disappear. The little man came out of the house and looked up in panic at his sky, shaking his tiny fist in anger at Janet.

Martin hummed a jaunty little tune to himself and wondered what was for dinner. The little man ran to his car, swearing and cursing. He drove away, with a sad look on his face. He'd almost got to the edge of the island, he'd almost got away, when Janet upended the kettle and flooded the whole place. She turned away and gave Martin a wide smile.

"There," she said, not looking back as a small blue car floated within the water, a tiny hand fluttering against the window. "That's done."

Martin nodded.

"Come on, Martin," she said, holding out her hands. "I'll let you watch me do the washing up."

Martin got up with a sigh, wondering whether he was going to be murdered with that fishbowl. It was definitely heavy enough to cave his head in, definitely not just light enough to cause the coma he'd been dreaming off.

He stood in the kitchen, watching Janet doing the

washing up, and wondered what Geoff and Linda did on a Saturday night.

~

Christie Cluett's Biography

Christie writes comedy fiction and is currently making the final edits to her first novel, a dark comedy about anxiety and trying to be normal.

She's one of the founding members of Stokes Croft Writers. She's meant to be writing but she's got a new puppy. She likes to judge.

~

Christie's Competition Judging Comments

I'm very honoured to have been a judge of this competition from its birth and, cliché though it is, I'm so impressed at the quality of writing that we get in every year. The longlist should be very proud of themselves.

It was very stiff competition this year. Most of the time, I forgot I was judging as I was so immersed in some really exceptional storytelling.

YOU HAVE MAIL

Judge's story, by Steph Minns

The rain was getting heavier and Milly wondered if she should call it a day and head home. Then she spotted the reconditioned laptop in the window of the dingy electrical bargain store she found herself outside, and decided this was just what she needed.

"The hard drive is wiped and re-formatted," the shopkeeper assured her. "It's got a three-month warranty too. Any problems, bring it right back."

So, the slightly scratched Purity 7 series went home

with Milly and she spent the rest of the rainy afternoon setting it up. She didn't have an email address and had so far only dabbled with the internet on her daughter's laptop, being late to the game at the tender age of 62.

Her daughter had insisted on signing her up for broadband, so Milly knew she had no excuse now. She applied for a free email account, set herself up as 'madnanna' and created her password, 'earlgreytea'. *The grandkids will be proud of my efforts*, she thought, *and they can send me pictures of all their pets now.*

Milly was taking a break, making toast, when the laptop pinged. *Who would be sending me emails?* she thought. *I haven't given anyone the address yet.*

Curious, she pressed the email button and opened it up.

Milly, I can see you.

That was the curious statement in the message. Feeling a little puzzled, she peered round the room and squinted back at the laptop as though it were some exotic and slightly naughty pet that just wouldn't settle. It was an old model and didn't have the camera eye her daughter's had at the top of the screen. *So, who is seeing me?* she thought. *Or is it some prank?*

She called her daughter, baffled.

"Maybe the guy at the shop put some spyware or something onto the hard drive, tracked that you've set up a new email account and hacked it," she offered helpfully. "There are all sorts of creepy, weird people about online."

She wasn't so sure. How did he know the family called her Milly, when the bank card she'd paid with said she was A. Sanders? A for Amelia.

As she ended the call, the laptop pinged again.

I hate you, you old baggage. Old people make me

sick, they should be wiped off the planet... old... old and fucking useless.

Shocked, she stepped back. Another message popped up immediately.

Look at you, with that blue granny cardigan, your fucking pearls, your old lady slippers. Disgusting. Bet you've had your big knickers on for days, stained with piss. Old people stink. They really wind me up.

"I have not got big knickers on," Milly said indignantly, then felt foolish for speaking out loud to a machine, as though somehow it, or someone somewhere, could hear her. But 'it' was right in some respects. She glanced down at herself. She was wearing a blue cardigan and had a pearl necklace on, fake pearls mind you. She marched over to the window to peer outside, expecting to see someone scuttle away. The front garden was empty.

The next ping brought a vile string of swear words and more abuse about old people, fingering granny fannies, more taunts about incontinence pads and dementia. Gathering her courage, Milly typed back a one-finger reply.

Who are you and how can you see me?

The next few minutes passed in tense silence, then the ping. Milly's stomach clenched in anticipation as she opened the mail.

I'm standing by the kitchen door, witch.

She spun round, expecting to see an intruder, but there was no one there.

Ping.

In the doorway, grandma. I'm a ghost. Whooo.

Alarmed, she pressed the power button and slammed the lid down, then pulled the plug from the socket.

"That shopkeeper has some explaining to do," she muttered angrily.

But she was nervous, uneasy, studying the empty kitchen door.

When an almighty crash came from the kitchen, she rushed in there to see what had happened. All the cups had crashed from the shelf above the sink to shatter on the floor. Not just fallen, these had flown the width of the kitchen with some force, the china shards piled up against the cabinet opposite. Milly drew in a sharp breath. Standing, staring at the carnage, she became aware of being watched; that creepy eyes-on-you feeling you sometimes get in a crowd. Then came the sharp tug on her hair, as though someone had twined cold fingers into the hair at the back of her head and spitefully pulled.

Milly let out an indignant yell. Darting for the front room, she was sure she heard a malicious chuckling just behind her. The laptop started frantically pinging messages again.

"But I pulled the plug out," she muttered, grabbing her coat from the bannister and heading out of the house. As she turned to close the front gate behind her, she was certain she saw a face at the front room window, watching her leave from behind the nets. It was only for a brief second or two, but she knew she'd seen it, a white face with a twisted, sneering grin and black sockets for eyes. A young man wearing a black hoodie had been gloating at her fearful retreat.

She sat for a long time at the bus stop, watching the rain slide its serpentine pathway down the acrylic panelling as she debated what to do next. What do you do with a granny-hating ghost in your home?

*

The rain had stopped by the time she reached the shop. The man who had served her looked startled as she marched in and demanded, "Who owned that second hand laptop I bought this morning? Where did it come from? I'm sure it's haunted."

She thought she must have sounded like a mad woman, and the shopkeeper looked uneasy when he replied, not meeting her gaze.

"Well, I don't know much, just that it was in a pile of gadgets brought in last week by a lad who said they'd belonged to his flat mate. His friend died, he said, during a car chase with police a short while back, in August I think, down on Zevier Street."

"Dead? What was he wanted for?" Milly asked.

"Er, I'll do a search in the local news, if you like?"

Tapping on his own laptop on the counter, he came back with a response almost immediately.

"Assault and robbery in a block of old folks sheltered flats, apparently."

"Oh, what you'd call a granny-basher, then." Milly frowned. "Easy targets, so he thought. I'll be bringing that laptop back for a refund tomorrow."

Milly was clear on what she would do now.

*

The chill hit her as soon as she stepped into the front room. She could almost see her breath misting as she shrugged off her coat. *Fight bullies at their own game,* she thought. *Taste of his own medicine, that's what.*

"I know you're here, you little scroat," Milly shouted towards the kitchen. A dark shadow-figure flitted past the doorway. He was listening.

"What have you got to say for yourself? Eh? If you were my grandson..."

Boldy, Milly took off her blue cardigan, but didn't stop there. Off came the dress, tights, bra. She just kept her nearly big knickers on, her sagging breasts swinging against the string of fake pearls as she stomped into the kitchen, where this kid seemed to like to hang out.

"Likin' what you see, son?" she demanded sarcastically. "Well, if you plan hanging around here, you'll have to get used to it. Me and my late husband, Cyril, were life-long nudists. Not much fazes me and some skinny dead kid sure as hell ain't going to scare me out of me own home. So get used to it."

The vague black mist seemed to gather itself into a corner by the cooker before shooting out through the back door. Milly smiled a smug smile of satisfaction and went back to the front room to put her clothes back on.

"Betting you won't be back, me lad."

~

Steph Minns' Biography

Steph has been a keen story writer and artist since childhood. Originally from the suburbs of London but now living in Bristol, UK, she works part-time as an administrator and spends her spare time writing. Her dark fiction stories range from ghost tales to urban and folk horror, and paranormal crime thrillers.

Her professional publishing history runs to several short stories, published by Grinning Skull Press, Almond Press and Zombie Pirate Publishing, among others. Also, a novella published by Dark Alley Press. Her latest novel is a paranormal crime thriller called *Death Wears A Top*

Hat, published by J. Ellington Ashton Press. She has also self-published a collection of short horror stories, *The Obsidian Path*, which has attained 5 star reviews on Amazon.

Steph is a member of Stokes Croft Writers, a small fiction writing group who host story-telling events around Bristol.

You can find more details on her website, where you can read free stories, interviews and reviews.

Website: www.stephminns.wixsite.com/author

Facebook: www.facebook.com/stephminnsfiction/

Amazon: www.amazon.co.uk/Steph-Minns/e/B00JNBQGP0

~

Steph's Competition Judging Comments

I found it really hard to choose one story over another, to be honest. There was so much good stuff and some great characters and settings popped out of the pages. My favourite genre is mystery and horror, but I really enjoyed these. Some shone when it came to plot, others on characterisation and dialogue. But eventually, the top three emerged for me.

My advice for new writers is plug away at sending your stuff out to competitions, websites looking for stories, and direct submissions to mags in your genre. Even if you're not a winner here, you will be somewhere.

ZOMBIES ON DIETS

Judge's story, by Mel Ciavucco

"Do you want to look as good as me?" said the man on TV with muscles that looked as if they were about to bulge through his skin.

Zoe, slumped on the sofa, sighed. It was the 12th times she'd seen this advert today. Dave, sitting on the sofa next to her, continued pushing snacks into his gaping mouth as he stared blankly at the screen.

"You want biceps? You want abs? Want a giant

package the size of mine?" The man on the TV grinned, grabbing his crotch. "Well, we've got a 15% discount for zombies today. Just promise you won't try and eat me. I'm pure muscle." He flexed his bicep.

Zoe grabbed the remote and snapped off the TV. "Bloody humans."

"Brains," shouted Dave next to her, still with a mouthful of brain snacks.

She knew she couldn't fool him, he could obviously tell they were only brain flavoured crisps, not made from real brains. He continued staring at the blank screen. "Brains."

"Eat your crisps," she said, wearily.

"Brains," he spat.

"No, Dave. We're fleshetarians now, remember?"

"Brains."

"No. Only flesh. And then we'll have to give that up too. I don't want to either, but what can we do? It's running out, Dave."

"Brains. Brains. Brains. Brains."

Zoe pushed herself up carefully, trying not to accidentally snap her wrist again. She couldn't take it. The other evening he'd chanted, "Brains," all night. She couldn't keep trying to trick him with these silly synthetic snacks. But it wasn't just Dave that missed that lovely nutty, grainy texture of real brains. Just thinking about it, she started to salivate. Drool seeped out of the corner of her cracked lips.

She hoped that one day they'd adapt to a flesh and brain-free diet, like the people on the TV were always telling them to. Human meat was in such short supply now. She blamed her parents' generation for draining all the supplies. They'd gotten overexcited, attacked and ate loads of humans without a single thought for the future. It's not that Zoe particularly liked humans. In fact, she hated them, with their stupid smug limbs that stayed attached and joints that worked. She especially hated the ones on the TV. They were the elite, protected from the clutches of zombies, living on secret islands. Only the strongest and fittest humans had survived; personal trainers, professional dancers, athletes, Beyoncé, and somehow the cast of *Love Island*. They all seemed to live in a smug world of glitz and cameras, constantly celebrating how they'd survived the zombie apocalypse.

There were still some humans left on the mainland but they were getting harder to find and Zoe didn't have the energy or strength to go hunting for the hiders. One human brain could last them both a short time if they rationed it carefully.

She went to the fridge and took out the Tupperware box containing the last little piece of brain from a man they killed three days ago. *We'd better eat it*, she thought. *Three-day rule and all that.* She went back into the lounge with two forks, with the intention of sharing the tiny bit of brain with Dave. As soon as he saw it, he grabbed it out of the Tupperware box and put the whole thing in this mouth.

"Dave, what did you do?"

"Brains," he moaned in joy.

Zoe would have cried if she hadn't been a zombie and unable to cry. That would have been the last bit of brain she would ever eat. She wanted to savour it. She couldn't do this anymore. Dave was out of control. They needed help.

*

Scrolling through Facebook, every other post was an advert. Musclemen off the TV promising to make you stronger. Creams to make your skin look human. Surgery to stop your limbs falling off, or to replace lost limbs. Stomach stapling to take away the urge for brains, or drugs to suppress the appetite. All human-made. Then suddenly, there was Sandra.

"Brain-free diets not working out for you?" Sandra asked her audience. She was wearing a big, puffy, pink dress with a huge headpiece in the shape of a bow, covered with rhinestones and glitter. Her eyebrows were drawn on most of the way up her forehead, and her eyeshadow was glittering pink and purple. But her drooping, grey skin and sunken eyes gave away the fact that she was indeed a zombie. Zoe watched carefully. She'd never seen an advert with a real zombie in it.

"Finding fleshetarianism a drag?" giggled Sandra. "Well, I can make those cravings go away, help you lose those extra pounds, and make you one of the good guys. Linda hasn't killed a single human in over three months, and she's dropped three dress sizes." An image of Linda holding up her old trousers flashed up on screen. "Well done, Linda. Do you want to be like Linda? Get in touch today."

Zoe emailed immediately. She definitely wanted to be like Linda.

*

Sandra ran a group down at the local community centre once a month on Monday evenings. Zoe dragged Dave along, following signs through the various doors and corridors until they found the correct room. Sandra was there, wearing a full sequin gown and a huge, pink, curly wig. There were eight other people sitting down, all miserable-looking fat zombies, some with limbs, some without.

"Hello, my darlings," Sandra cried, reaching out her arms towards them. "Come on in, don't be shy. We don't bite, well, not each other." She let out a sharp burst of laughter, then stopped and gave them a stern look. "Sit down over there."

With that, she walked out of the room.

Zoe turned to the man next to her who was slumped in his chair. "Where's she going?"

"Oh, she does this every time. She's going to walk into the room very dramatically and we all have to stand up and clap and whistle. If you can whistle. I can't whistle, my lips will crack."

Then Sandra waltzed back into the room, doing a little twirl. The zombies rose to their feet as best they could and clapped half-heartedly. Someone attempted a whistle.

"Oh, thank you. How unexpected," beamed Sandra. "Now sit down."

She gave Zoe a pile of handouts and told her to pass them around. On it was a list of 'good' foods and 'bad' foods. Next to the 'bad' column was a picture of an unhappy, fat zombie. Next to the 'good' was a happy smiling zombie, that almost looked human. Zoe had never seen a zombie like that in her life.

"Today we've got some newbies, so we're going to have a little reminder of good and bad foods. It seems some of you have probably been pigging out on brains again, but I guess we'll find out for sure when we do the weigh-in." Her tone was now stern and unfriendly. "So, can somebody tell me, without looking at the handout, what the bad foods are?"

Silence. Zoe kept her head down.

"Brains," said Dave. Zoe snapped her head round to look at him, then realised she'd moved a little bit too fast and clutched her neck.

"Well done, new guy," said Sandra. "Anything else?"

"Brains. Brains. Brains."

"Oh, he's a one word-er. Brilliant."

"Sorry," Zoe started, "he's alright really..."

"Shush. Unless you're going to tell me what the other bad food is?"

"Flesh?" Zoe said, tentatively.

"Yes. See? Even the newbies are better than you lot," she told the rest of the group. "And so what are the good foods?"

Silence.

Sandra sighed. "Fine. Water, bananas, asparagus – the sticks can have the texture of fingers sometimes so that's nice – and of course any officially registered fleshetarian foods, including the new microwaveable brain pie. Mmm, tasty," she said with over-enthusiasm.

All those foods were manufactured by humans. Zoe had purposely come to see this woman thinking that it would involve something that wasn't human-made, but this was clearly just a farce.

"OK, time for the weigh-ins," Sandra said, clapping her hands together. She glanced at Zoe and Dave. "I won't be mean and make you go first," she told them. "OK, just kidding. I will."

Zoe looked at her for a moment, unsure if she was joking.

"I'm not joking," Sandra told her. "Get on the scales."

Zoe got up, suddenly feeling exposed, and shuffled to the scales. She carefully stepped up on them.

Sandra started tutting and shaking her head. "Well, well. You must be the fattest zombie we've had here in a while. You've been gorging on brains, haven't you?"

"Well... erm, I've really been trying not to," Zoe stuttered. "I've been trying to buy all the fleshetarian snacks but they're expensive. And Dave... well, he just loves brains so much."

"What a bloody cop-out," Sandra cried. "Blaming your poor husband. What a terrible thing to do. Sit down, you stupid fat cow."

"I... I..." Zoe wanted to knock that silly wig off her head. She wanted to scrape the glitter off her face and tear her fancy sequin dress to pieces. But she couldn't speak or move. She felt a deep ache in her chest, and her cheeks felt flushed even though that was impossible.

"Brains," shouted Dave, suddenly getting up from his seat and staggering over to Zoe and Sandra. "Brains, brains, brains."

"It's OK, Dave," said Zoe, "sit back down. I'll be alr—"

Before she could finish the sentence, Dave punched Sandra in the face. Zoe looked down at Dave's hand as all his fingers fell off. Dave pointed at Sandra with his other hand. She was struggling to get up, knocked off her platform heels.

"BRAINS," he said, urgently.

Zoe, understanding exactly what her husband meant, snatched off Sandra's wig. Underneath was a pink, bald head, encasing what could only be a beautiful human brain.

"She's human," said Zoe.

She looked around the room at the others, who were still sitting in shock. "She's bloody human, honestly."

"No, no, I'm not," pleaded Sandra. "I'm a zo—"

Zoe had already smashed a chair into her head. Her skull split open and juicy brains came out. In merely a moment, the entire room was fighting over Sandra's brains. When every last bit had been eaten, Zoe felt compelled to address the room.

"The humans have clearly been sending people in, masquerading as zombies, to trick us into buying and eating their crap." She was jabbing her finger into the air, getting louder with every word. "Do any of you actually know any zombies who survive purely on these so-called *good* foods?"

The zombies shook their heads solemnly.

"Exactly. It's because we can't survive without brains and flesh, and the humans know this and it's their plot to kill us off. We have to stop them. We are zombies. We are higher in the food chain than them. We need to find them and we need to eat all of their brains."

"Brains," shouted Dave with his fist in the air.

"Brains, brains, brains," the zombies chanted as they marched out of the room.

*

As soon as Zoe got home, she set up a secret Facebook group inviting all the zombies she knew, explaining the plan and encouraging them to get every single zombie they knew involved. They were building an army. They were going to find the island on which the humans were living and eat their brains. She'd done some Googling and she was quite sure that many of them were hiding out on the Isle of Wight.

*

It wasn't quite an army, but Zoe had gathered at least 16 zombies. They'd stolen a boat and were on their way to the Isle of Wight.

"So, why do you think they're on the Isle of Wight?" one of the zombies asked Zoe.

"Well, it's close enough to keep control of us, but far enough away to be safe. Or so they think. Plus, this is probably the furthest we can go without getting caught, or keeling over from malnutrition. We're all starving, guys, and it's the humans' fault. They've got to pay."

"Yes," they all cheered.

"Brains," added Dave.

"I hope Beyoncé is there," one of the young female zombies said.

"Would you really want to eat her brains, if you like her?"

"I'd make her do a few songs first, then I'd eat her brains," said the young woman.

Zoe rolled her eyes. In truth, she didn't know what to expect from this mission. But she knew they had to do something or they were going to die very soon. They couldn't let the humans control them anymore.

As they approached the shore, they could see people. Real people; humans with brains. The zombies all started licking their lips, gurgling with excitement.

"We did it," Zoe said. "There are humans here."

"I can't see Beyoncé," the young zombie sighed.

They arrived at the port and tied up the boat. She couldn't see any humans now. Zoe assumed they'd all run inside to hide.

The zombies descended on the nearest houses, slowly, with the little energy they had. They opened the doors to find clusters of very attractive people in skimpy swimwear. Zoe went to bite into a woman's arm but the skin was rubbery and wouldn't break. The woman simply smiled at her. Zoe smashed a glass against her head and cut open her skull only to find... nothing. Zoe turned her over and found what looked like a microchip in the back of the neck.

"Dammit. They're robots."

"Oh, I recognise them now," said the young female zombie. "It's the cast of *Love Island*."

"Shit," said Zoe, as her own arm fell off and Dave's head dropped off next to her.

~

Mel Ciavucco's Biography

Mel Ciavucco is a writer, editor and vlogger from the UK. She writes and talks about body image and gender equality, as well as writing fiction.

Mel is passionate about writing stories that challenge social norms, showcase diverse characters and contain realistic portrayals of mental health. She believes that sharing our stories and stepping out of our comfort zones makes us all better human beings.

Website: www.melciavucco.weebly.com

Twitter: @MCiavucco

Facebook: www.facebook.com/melciavuccowriter

Instagram: www.instagram.com/melciavucco

~

Mel's Competition Judging Comments

It's To Hull And Back time again — 20 awesome stories, all so different and brilliant in their own right.

I love judging this competition, but it's never easy to pick a winner. From the quirky reads to the darker, subtly comedic stories, I enjoyed each and every one.

Congratulations to all the writers, and thank you to Chris Fielden for making this happen.

A FINAL NOTE

Thank you to all the writers who entered the competition and everyone that purchases this anthology. Your continued support allows To Hull And Back to grow and bring more attention to humorous writing.

While you wait for the next competition, why not take part in my writing challenges? They're all free to enter, every submission is published and money from book sales are donated to charity. Check them out here: www.christopherfielden.com/writing-challenges/

Until next time ☺

Chris Fielden

Printed in Great Britain
by Amazon

77317860R00153